Identity & Dignity

How Walking Away Paralyzed from Abuse Paved my Path of Soul-Discovery

A memoir of

Hawa Makhawa

All names and cities have been changed to protect the privacy of individuals.

Photograph: Pascal Mathieu
Painting: L' Artiste Txica

This is my story and every word is true.

Contents

Prologue

Humans have forgotten that there was once a time when they talked with the animals. Yet in Gaya, this ancestral connection between species could sometimes still be found. One night, as I was sleeping with my brothers and sisters outside under the full moon, I woke up to find my friend, the talking dog, was there. He is one of those yellow dogs that are common in that part of the world, with ears that are a little too large and lined with black. He is quite small and has a pointed muzzle and is as skinny as a bag of bones – a dog without a master that hangs out between the desert and the city. He used to visit me from time to time, but that night he had come to say goodbye. "There is no room here for animals anymore," he told me. "No, please don't go!" I cried. But he turned to the moon, gave me one last glance and fled into the night. Years later, I asked my big brother if the dog still came to visit. He laughed and told me that he was the one who had told me that story. Yet last night, away from Gaya and those dreamy nights, the dog came back. This time, he was waiting for me under the German moon. So, I went out to talk to him.

The yellow dog asked me to tell him my story, but I did not know how. I am trying to live another life now, the life that I have chosen, and lifting the curtain of memory is painful. But I know that the dog has come to lift the veil that covers my chest and threatens to smother me until I sometimes choke. Our interview, which took place on the hill, under the complicit light of the moon, lasted until daybreak.

CHAPTER 1

Gaya

The yellow dog: Tell me about life in Gaya.

Gaya is a city in the northeast of Mali bordered by the Sahara Desert and the Niger River. It is known for Kalouma, the Purple Dune, which lies directly on the riverbank. The dune has a shallow slope on the town side, while the other side falls steeply into the river. For the inhabitants this is a miracle because it prevents the city being flooded by the river. Gaya developed into an important trade crossroads and became a center of trans-Saharan commerce. In the 15th and 16th centuries, the Songhai Empire was located there, ruled over by the Sonni dynasty, which still characterizes the town today.

Everyday life in Gaya was marked by poverty. People learned to help each other to survive. The houses were made of clay and the landscape was bare and sandy. There was hardly any green vegetation because there were regular periods of drought. The farm animals roamed freely, and it was common for people to keep livestock for their own purposes. I can still remember seeing donkey carts everywhere.

Mali is a Muslim country and life there was shaped by religion and tradition. Most marriages were arranged, which meant families needed bride money. In my memories of life in Gaya, I possessed only one pair of old, dirty and torn underpants. I do not know whether

I ever had other garments there. It is normal to wear a boubou and turban. A boubou is a loose-fitting, embroidered garment made of cotton. They are dyed in various colors and sewn by hand. Usually this robe is worn by men, but in Mali there is a variant for women that is also worn on special occasions. Mali was famous for its embroidered boubous throughout the Dark Continent.

When I return to Gaya, I always feel that time stopped just after the birth of Jesus! Of my city, I remember only the neighborhood where I lived. Ours was a traditional compound and we lived there with my uncle and aunt. There was a faucet in the compound, which was a luxury at that time. To me, our house looked sad. It was very simple and made of clay. Before I fell ill, I used to sleep with all my brothers and sisters on the same mattress. Whoever got there first took the best place! We also slept outside if it was too hot. There were seven of us children before I left Mali and now we are eleven. There was another child, my mother's first, but she had a miscarriage. Nevertheless, she always says, "You are twelve."

My father was an important man in the neighborhood. He ran a store that faced the street. At first he sold goods, and vegetables that he grew in a garden. We were not allowed to eat his vegetables. I remember once I took a tomato because I was hungry, and he was very angry with me. Years later, after the shop closed down, that was where my father hid all the toys and clothes I sent them. In Gaya, I was always hungry! At mealtimes, we kids were given the leftovers. I was small, and I was too slow, but fortunately, my big brother always kept a little food for me.

When I think of my mother, my head smokes! She is a very beautiful woman, but cold as ice. Ever since I could think, I had the feeling that she hated me. Maybe I was just too small to remember a mother's love. I try to remember good times with her. Once she gave me a boubou with bracelets, and I also have a small basket that she gave me. I once tried to kiss her, but she refused. When I was a teenager, I missed her so much that I idealized her. It is because of her that I have the piercing in my nose. Back then, if she had wished, I would have done anything to bring her to Germany. But she asked for a television instead. And now she is asking me for a laptop and cell phone. Last time I visited Gaya, I saw her holding my younger sister in her arms and I was amazed and jealous, because I can't remember her ever holding me. To understand her, I am obliged to look at her history. I do not know everything, but enough to know that she too is a victim of the traditions and rules imposed by a society dominated by men. She never knew she could change her life, yet she possesses extraordinary strength. She managed to raise her family without the help of my father. When he had money, he kept it for himself. While we went to bed on an empty stomach, he went into town to enjoy himself. He would disappear for weeks at a time, leaving my mother to fend for herself. She sometimes fell out with our neighbor because she was unable to return what she had borrowed from her. She had a very hard life and I think she does not know what it is to love, to have emotions, because she did not experience those things herself when she was small. I think that is probably why she hides in material things.

I wonder whether, if my mother had been different, I would also be a different person today. She certainly passed on her strength to her children in her own way. She gave us the essentials: life itself.

According to tradition at that time in Gaya, when a child was born, a feast for the newborn would be held a few days after the birth. Members of the extended family shared their joy and gratitude to Allah and an animal was slaughtered. This Islamic custom is called Aqiqah and is a happy occasion. When my baby brother was born, everyone was excited about the feast day. I watched the hustle and bustle and could not understand the excitement: He was just a baby boy, after all! I was looking forward to the food though, because finally we would get to eat well: lamb meat, salads and various traditional dishes. As I was only in the way, I was constantly sent back and forth and was not allowed to touch anything until the beginning of the celebration.

Slowly, the first guests started to arrive, and the house filled up. Everyone was dressed nicely and smelled fresh. I don't remember what I wore that day, or what happened to me exactly. But I remember the tall man in a blue robe and turban. I wondered who he was and where he had come from. He talked with my mother for a very long time. At one point, my mother realized I was watching them and looked at me strangely, as if I was worthless. I could tell they were talking about me and planning something. My mother brought the man to the table next to me, said something incomprehensible and went back. My little sister was sitting next to me on the floor and we were playing. The man entertained us. He made us laugh. And then he took me away somewhere. I don't know what happened. After that I only had nightmares. I did not want my mother to touch me or be near me. I can remember that my mother once got into trouble with my father, because he did not want her to touch me either. I no longer know how old I was at that time – maybe two or three? There were no birth certificates in Gaya when I was born. My birth certificate was created later, when I was living in Germany. Even my parents do not really know how old they are. Their ages were only ever an estimate.

After the Aqiqah incident, I clung to my aunt Niara, my father's younger sister. She was mixed-race because her father was a Frenchman. She was quite a bit smaller than my father and one of the few Europeans in Gaya at that time. Niara and I became inseparable. After that event I always ate with her and slept close to her. In her arms I felt protected and safe. Niara always told me beautiful stories – that one day I would marry a wonderful man, that God had great plans for me and that this was the reason I was being tested. Niara was very devout, and she told me that no matter what happened, I should never be mad at the Lord. I liked listening to her, although I did not know what she meant.

CHAPTER 2

Poison

The yellow dog: How did you end up paralyzed?

A short time after the Aqiqah feast, my parents had to have me vaccinated. I did not want to be vaccinated. I had a weird feeling about it. I told my father that the doctor was going to hurt me and that something bad would happen to me if we went there, but he just laughed. I could not sleep for days beforehand. On the day of the vaccination, I kept hiding and inventing excuses so I wouldn't have to go. My father played along with me until the evening and then he became very angry and grabbed me by the hand and dragged me to the doctor.

The closer we got to the practice, the worse I felt. I would have liked to sink into the ground. In the doctor's room, I hid and pulled away from the syringe. After a while, the doctor yelled at me and my father did too. He held me tightly so the doctor could give me the vaccination. This syringe was huge. It looked like a pistol and the needle looked like a diamond drill. After that, I was very angry with my father. I stopped talking to him, although he was very friendly to me. The next day I did not feel well. I became quieter and more withdrawn. I felt different.

A few days later, my father picked me up from the day care center on his moped. I was not feeling well. The strange feeling had become stronger and more powerful. My bones ached so much. A strong heat came up in me, yet at the same time I was freezing. I sat on the moped, but my father quickly realized that something was different. I was unusually quiet. We drove off, but before we reached our house, the chain broke. I got off and sat down on the ground while he tried to repair the chain. Suddenly I started to freeze under the blazing sun and my whole body trembled. My father was busy with the moped and did not realize that my condition had worsened. When he finally finished, he called me to come, but I could not move. I was shaking. I was cold and hot at the same time and my teeth were chattering. My father called again. I knew I was supposed to move but I could not. Then he turned to me and saw me trembling. He came to me and tried to pull me up onto my feet, but I kept falling down again. I could not feel my left leg. It wasn't responding, and I was too weak to stand on the other one. My father took me in his arms and ran home with me. There he laid me down and I fell asleep. When I woke up the next day, I could not feel my legs anymore. They were both unresponsive and I couldn't control them.

A short time later, I got a high fever and fell asleep again. I began to dream. I was in a special place, where I learned and played with children and adults. This place was out of this world. Sometimes something pulled me out of this place and I saw a woman kneeling and crying in front of a person lying down. She was praying all the time. Since it did not mean anything to me, I went back to the beautiful place, where everything was harmonious and peaceful. This back and forth carried on for a long time before I realized that the crying woman was my mother and the person lying down was me.

My mother was suffering. I could feel that clearly. The time had come for me to make a decision: Should I stay there or here? I spoke with my friends in the special place and, together, we decided that it would be best to go back. My new friends promised me that they would always be there for me. Then I woke up slowly and I was alone in the room.

After that, my dear aunt Niara and Kouami, my favorite older brother, took care of me. The bond with my aunt became even closer. My aunt and my brother did everything for me, and my other siblings and even my mother became friendly towards me for a while. Later I found out that I had been in a coma for a couple of weeks and my mother was afraid she was going to lose me the whole time and prayed every day at my bedside for healing. I was glad that this vision had not been a dream. I took it as a sign that my mother must love me.

When I got better, I could not walk, so I started to crawl. I did not want to go to the day care center anymore because I could not play the way I used to and I was ashamed of crawling. I started to hide, or scream like a wild hen when people called me or touched me. At that time, I only trusted two people: Kouami and Niara. Kouami always made me laugh to distract me from negative feelings. And my aunt made sure that I sometimes got a wheelchair on loan from the hospital. The wheelchair was huge and I was small and dainty and kept falling out of it, so they had to strap me in.

One day, Kouami took me out with him on the moped. Because I could no longer control my legs, I had to hold on to him with my hands. Somehow, my legs got tangled in the wheels. I shouted for him to stop, but he didn't hear me immediately. When he saw what had happened he was very sorry and fetched help right away.

After the accident, I fell into a long deep sleep. When I woke up, I was in a lot of pain. I lifted my head and saw my bloody legs, which were bright red because most of the skin was gone. I howled and Kouami came running to comfort me. He kept apologizing but I could not be angry with him and I forgave him quickly because I knew it was an accident. He nursed me and played with me and I loved him even more than before.

Meanwhile, I had to get used to crawling on the stony and sandy ground that ripped the skin on my legs and hands. After my paralysis, my brother gave me a separate plate to eat from. Before that, we all used to eat from one large bowl using our right hand. The men ate first, and then the boys. The wives and girls had to share the leftovers.

A short time later, a tall, light-skinned man came to visit with a strange-looking woman. He had golden hair and extremely blue eyes and the woman was smaller than my mother, and her hair was dark and fine. The couple introduced themselves as Frank and Fabienne. Frank was German and Fabienne was French. At that time, I did not even know there were any places outside of Gaya. When I first saw this white man with golden hair and extremely bright blue eyes, my whole body started to tremble. I had never seen anyone who looked different from us before and something told me that this man would take me with him, just like the man who appeared during our Aqiqah feast. I quickly hid behind my mother and I said to her, "See, the devil is coming to fetch me." She just laughed and said "No." Soon after, my father, my mother and my big sister took me to the camp-site where Frank and Fabienne were staying. It was full of strange things we had never seen before: cars, gas cookers, music players and dresses. They gave me a Bobby Car. I was happy but also sad because I could not ride on it myself and I was afraid the others would take it away from me. I have no idea what happened to it, even now. The afternoon was nice, but the uneasy feeling I had was getting stronger. I was glad when the couple left because then I knew that I would be staying with my family. When they came to say goodbye, they saw a big bump on my baby brother's forehead and insisted on taking him to the hospital. I was very worried about him when he was gone, but they brought him back with a thick white bandage on his forehead and he seemed better than before and that made me happy. Still, I was relieved when the cars drove away.

I did not know then that Fabienne was unable to have children, or that my father, when he heard this, had said, "I have one for you. She is disabled."

CHAPTER 3

Togo

The yellow dog: How was your first trip to Volta and what happened there?

A few months later, the two strangers, Frank and Fabienne, came back again. Frank said to my father that he had spoken to a German doctor in Volta who said that I probably had polio. Frank said the doctor could help me, but he would have to take me to Volta for the treatment. Of course, my father agreed. They wanted only the best for me – or that's what I thought for years. I was distraught though because I knew I would not come back. How was I supposed to get along without my family? I thought I must have done something bad and now I was being punished for it.

My father was very happy and he took my three older brothers with us on the trip by bus from Gaya to Volta. It was a very exciting trip for me and my siblings, as we had never travelled before. I remember that on this trip I saw a scorpion and I wanted to play with it. My father, who was being attentive for once, picked me up quickly and explained the danger. For me, this moment between father and daughter was an important gesture of love.

The journey to Volta took us through Burkina Faso and Benin. Unfortunately, my memory of this trip is not clear, because I was too small and I was distracted. I was already missing my aunt, my little sister and my little brother. Everything was new and overwhelming.

It was nighttime when we arrived in Volta. It had rained recently and the air still smelled of earth. We stayed in a house with a beautiful garden. I had never seen so many plants and colorful flowers before. It was very different from Gaya. I took a deep breath and let it go with a loud sigh.

The next day, Frank took us to the sea. On the way there I observed my new surroundings from the window. We drove on an asphalt road. The ground to the left and right of it was sandy and busy with people. There were many small shops, food stalls, restaurants and hotels. When I first saw the sea, my eyes shone. The salty air rushed up my nose and I felt the cool breeze on my face. I just sat on the beach because I didn't know how to swim, but I enjoyed the day at the seaside very much.

Soon after we got back to the house, I developed a high fever. My big brother Kouami took care of me as usual. Over the following days, Frank and my father arranged the necessary documents for me. When I got well again, they took me to the hospital. The doctors examined me and operated on me almost immediately. Everything happened way too fast and I did not know what to expect. When the anesthetic wore off, my legs hurt and I could not move at all because they were in plaster. I was all on my own in a large, cool room.

After a few days, another girl joined me in the room. She was older and had polio too. My family did not come to visit me until several days later and they did not stay long. I was in a lot of pain and kept crying out. My recovery was unexpectedly slow, so I was in the hospital for a few months. My family, Frank and Fabienne came to visit me only twice in that time. All these changes were very unexpected.

The mother of the girl in the next bed came to visit her every day and took care of her. She prayed constantly, massaged the girl's legs and brought her fresh food. After two or three weeks she recovered and left. Her mother said goodbye to me with the words, "If you just cry and do not pray to the Lord, you will never be healthy." That went straight to my heart! How was I supposed to pray when I was in such pain? Was it my fault my family was not as caring as this woman?

I felt so lonely. I had never been alone before. I wondered why there was no one to take care of me. I assumed the others were having fun while I was suffering. I only had my thoughts to occupy me. Time seemed like an eternity. Next to my bed was a window with bars from which I could look out onto the street. I watched the women preparing and selling delicious-smelling food. The road was crowded with people, cars and motorcycles. It was always noisy out there.

Once the plaster came off, the doctors fitted me with leg braces and I learned to walk a bit. When I started to walk, they discharged me, even though I was still in pain. I walked like a robot because the braces locked my joints. I wore a corset that reached all the way up to my shoulders and they gave me crutches to use. The corset on top of the braces was meant to bring my upper body into an upright position, since I had developed extreme scoliosis from crawling. Because I was still growing, crawling had distorted my joints and my small body.

When I left the hospital, Frank and my father brought me to a different house. I was sad because I had liked the first house with the garden. I had thought about it often in hospital and was looking forward to exploring it. A few days later, Frank and Fabienne drove with me and my family to the sea. I could hardly wait to see the sea again at last. It was so good to feel the warm sun and cool breeze on my skin again. After the beach, we drove to the market. The market was huge and crowded and the air was full of smells: fresh oranges, tomatoes, pastries, motor oil and sweat. Afterwards, Frank took us to a German restaurant.

My father and brothers stayed in Volta for a few more days. While my brother Kouami was there taking care of me, I was fine. But one morning I woke up and they had gone. They had driven away without saying goodbye. My world collapsed overnight. I found myself alone with two strange-looking people who claimed to be my new parents! These strangers were constantly taking me to offices and organizations.

CHAPTER 4

Frank and Fabienne

The yellow dog: How was life with your new parents?

In order to fit into this new life, sadly I had no choice but to forget my past experiences because remembering them was too painful. Suddenly, I was a long way from my family and home, living with strangers. What had I done? Was I a bad person? For a while, I thought I was dreaming and I would wake up soon and be back home with my family. Sometimes I thought if I stopped being angry with my mother, I would be able to go back. I apologized to her several times in my heart and thoughts, but nothing changed.

Eventually, I began to explore my new home. Everything here was so different from Gaya. I had my own room, clean clothes and quite a lot of toys. The house was very large. There were two courtyards and in one there was a horse. His name was Beauty and he was a black stallion with a white stripe on his forehead. Since I had never seen a horse before, I was afraid of him. There was a dog called Hexe that used to bite dark-skinned people because she had been abused by dark-skinned people when she was a puppy. Hexe and I were never really close. After a while, she learned to tolerate me but there was an invisible barrier between us that I was careful not to cross.

There was a parrot who could repeat anything you said and whistled prettily. The animals all belonged to Frank and he took good care of them. Hexe and Beauty were best friends and did everything together. Hexe loved to grab Beauty's tail and toss it in the air, like a kind of carousel.

Frank was a car dealer and mechanic. He was also passionate about riding and collecting motorcycles. Once I watched him sorting out his toolbox. I was curious and used hand gestures to ask him what he was doing and whether I could help. He explained everything to me and let me brush the tools. I was very happy. He gave me a stool and I put some plastic headphones on my head, because I had once seen a beautiful woman in a magazine listening to a Walkman and looking happy. I wanted to feel this feeling too, so I put the headphones on my head, closed my eyes and smiled as I brushed the tools.

Frank and I often played and laughed together in the beginning. And Fabienne also paid attention to me. She made sure that I was washed because she wanted me to look beautiful and well cared for. I quickly made friends with the neighbor's children, Koffi and Abla. They were brother and sister and lived opposite us. Abla was much older than me and Koffi. She was always quiet and a good older sister. Her hair was always braided back nicely, and she liked wearing knee-length dresses or skirts. Her little brother Koffi had very short hair and always wore shorts or pants. He was very lively and we got on immediately. Playing with them, I quickly picked up the local language, Mina, and French. From then on, we saw each other every day. They liked to come to my house because I loved sharing my toys. Hexe bit Abla and had to be locked away for a time, but after a while Hexe got used to her and, as long as Abla and Koffi kept their distance, everything was alright. Sometimes I went to their house. Nana, their mother, treated me like her own child. Nana was strong and witty and had her own hair salon.

Koffi and I looked very similar and people always thought we were twins. As a child I always had short hair and preferred to wear shorts, so I looked like a boy too. At that time, I wanted to be a boy, because I thought that boys suffered less. I thought I must be ugly because I figured no one would hurt a pretty child.

I went out with Frank and Fabienne a lot. Fabienne taught me to swim with her best friend Julienne. After I had mastered the children's pool, we went to the beach. I loved swimming in the sea. I loved the salty taste in my mouth and the fact that the waves kept coming and going as if they were playing.

There were lots of German, English, Dutch, Chinese and French people living in Volta at that time. And they all seemed to know one other. The country was not very big. Fabienne and Frank used to go out every night, so they hired a nanny to take care of me. She soon moved into the house and lived with us. Her name was Sophie. She was medium height and a bit plump, and she often braided her hair backwards. Her most striking trait was her protruding tooth. She was a very serious woman and never smiled. After Sophie´s arrival, I saw very little of Frank and Fabienne. In the beginning, Sophie just did her work: cooking, cleaning and taking care of me. She did not engage with me personally or get close to me, although we shared a room.

At this time, I used to wet the bed every night. Every night I dreamed of evil monsters who wanted to eat me up. Sophie was always annoyed because she had to change the bed every morning or in the middle of the night. I wanted to defeat the monsters in my dream. They were huge plush animals that wanted to eat me up and I hid from them. Later, I began to fight the monsters and one night they vanished. But I continued to wet the bed. Then I noticed that in my new dreams I always dreamt I had to go to the bathroom and each time I sat on the toilet in my dream, I wet the bed. Eventually, I worked out that if I dreamt I had to go the bathroom, I had to get up. I was so happy the first time I woke Sophie up so that she could take me to the bathroom. I never wet the bed again.

Frank and Fabienne were hardly ever there and at one point they went away. I had no idea where they were. Were they even still in Togo? Sophie brought her children into the house and we played together. They liked Koffi and Abla too.

I had never really liked the leg braces and corset because I could not play freely. They held me rigid and my hands were occupied with the crutches. Without the braces I had to crawl. So I crawled. As time went by, I became very nimble. I could almost run. I climbed trees and played hide-and-seek. This was a very happy time for me.

Every night before going to bed I thought of my family in Gaya, especially Niara. It was months since I'd last seen my father and brothers. Then one night at midnight I woke to find my father and my older brother Yusuf standing by my bed. I flung myself around my father's neck and he said, "Look who I've brought" and I saw Fanta, a friend of mine from Gaya. She had a very bad burn on her lower arm that had to be treated. I was sorry for her, and although I was happy to see my father and brother again, I could not go back to being the way I used to be with them because I didn't know how long they would stay. I was also aware that Frank must have gone to Gaya without telling me or taking me with him. I would have liked to see my entire family again.

Fanta's arm was treated the next day. I did not want her to suffer the same fate as me and hoped that her arm would recover so she could go home again. Fortunately, although the burn was serious, her arm did not have to be amputated. When she left with my father and brother, my father promised me that he would come back soon. From then on, I sat by the front door every night after school and waited for my father. On weekends I waited from morning to night. Weeks and months passed, but he never came. That was the last time I saw my father and brother in Togo.

Once again, my family had abandoned me and I cried every night. I decided to think only of my friends and my surroundings, because they did not hurt me. By then I could speak French and Mina very well. I could barely remember my mother tongue, Songhai. Frank brought a man from Gaya to talk to me in Songhai, but when he realized I could not speak it anymore, he got mad at me. The man was supposed to take me to school and pick me up again, but he left after a few days.

Frank changed a lot around this time. He was full of rage and hatred towards me. He yelled at me and started to forbid all sorts of things. He also wanted to hit me, but he was able to control himself then. I shrank even further inside myself and tried to avoid his temper. I cannot really remember Fabienne, my adoptive mother, at this time. When she was around, she no longer spent time with me, and she would only stay for a few hours and then disappear again for a while. All I had was my mind and my heart. There I could do anything I wanted and there was no one to hurt me. I used to imagine a more beautiful world and future. I wanted to be sweet, kind and pretty and have lots of nice people around me. Every night before I fell asleep, I said a short prayer and sent greetings to my family.

Frank was extremely strict with me. He forced me to wear the braces every day and made me do exercises that were supposed to help me walk again. He also started beating me. Once he beat me for days because of some chewing gum. The chewing gum was his and he told me not to take any. In the evening, he put it on the table and watched while I went to bed. In the morning, I got up, dressed and drank my glass of milk, and the driver took me to school. Frank picked me up from school. The moment he arrived, my whole body began to tremble. I could feel his rage. He kept himself in check until we got home. Then he accused me of stealing his chewing gum. I said I could not have done it since I'd only just come home from school. He said I'd stolen it in the morning. I said no, I didn't. He asked me to tell the truth. I said, "I did not take your chewing gum!" Suddenly he hit me with his fists several times and yelled at me, calling me a thief and a liar, and asking if that was how I repaid him for everything he had done for me. He beat me for a long time until Sophie told him to stop. I was in pain and lay on the floor crying my eyes out. Sophie carried me to bed and took care of me. The next morning, Frank started again. He asked me if I had taken his chewing gum. I said no, and *thwack* he hit me again. This time he took his shoe so he could hit me even harder. My whole body hurt. I couldn't lie on my back or sit down. I couldn't understand why I was being punished for telling the truth. Fabienne was there that morning too, sitting calmly on the couch and smoking.

Sophie's daughter took pity on me that evening and whispered that it was her brother who had taken the chewing gum. But after seeing what had happened to me, he was far too scared to admit what he had done. So what should I do? I did not want him to go through the same thing as me. The next day, Frank asked the same question and this time I said yes, because it seemed to make no difference whether I told the truth or not. This time he was even more violent than before – because I had lied to him! I was done with the world. I could not lie on my back for days. Sophie was genuinely sorry for me and took care of me. Suddenly, I had become more than just a job to her. Sometimes when Frank hit me, Sophie would call Nana to help me, because she was stronger than Frank. Nana would take me to her house and hold me. Sometimes Frank hit me so hard that Nana would hear me yelling and come running to save me.

Frank and Fabienne used to disappear for days or weeks at a time and then suddenly reappear for a few hours. I spent most of the time alone with Sophie at home. When they were there, they were cold towards me. They took me to parties and when I got tired, I would sleep at the party or in the car, which became my second home. Frank forgot to pick me up from school a few times. The school attendant called him to ask what he should do with me, because it was late. He told me someone would come and fetch me soon. But Frank didn't turn up until hours later and then he was mad at me because he had had to leave a party or a friend's house because of me. But if I caught a ride home with someone else, he would hit me for ruining his reputation. I never knew what to do in that situation.

In Volta, I celebrated Christmas for the first time. Frank and Fabienne put up a *sapin de Nöel*, a Christmas tree decorated with colorful lights, baubles and small gifts. They told me about Santa Claus and Fabienne read me Christmas stories. We ate very well and celebrated with Frank and Fabienne's friends. When I woke up and found lots of presents under the tree, I was very surprised. Fabienne told me they were all for me. After I had opened my beautiful gifts, we ate the *b*ûche de Nöel, a yule log with a chocolate coating and a cream filling. I had never tasted such a delicious cake before and even though I got stomachache after one piece, I couldn't stop eating. I was so happy.

People in Gaya did not know about Christmas, so then I became sad that my siblings were not there to celebrate with me. The next day I took a piece of pie to Koffi and Abla's house. I was looking forward to finding out what they had got from Santa Claus. When they saw the pie, they opened their eyes wide and said they had not been given anything! That made me very sad. I did not understand why I was the only one to get presents because the books said that Santa Clause gave gifts to all the children in the world. I read the books again and again. Suddenly, it occurred to me that he only went into the houses that had a chimney. Koffi and Abla's house didn't have a chimney, but neither did ours. I decided I didn't like Santa Claus anymore. I shared my toys with Koffi and Alba and gave some away as well, except for my books and Barbie dolls.

An older friend of Frank's, another German man, always reminded me of Santa Claus. He had white hair and his cheeks and nose were red. I asked Frank why that was, and he said it was because he drank so much beer. We both laughed at that. It made me think that Santa Claus was always drunk, and maybe that was why the others didn't get any presents. I thought they might arrive late, but they never did. Christmas seemed very unfair!

Fabienne laughed differently from everyone else. She showed her teeth and that always looked funny. I asked her why she laughed like that and she told me I should always show my teeth when laughing, no matter what anyone said. We used to practice in front of the mirror, but I did not want to show my teeth because I thought it looked odd. Fabienne started to teach me manners. I had to sit at the table with a straight back, keep my elbows off the table and hold my hand in front of my mouth if I burped. She was often not there and when she was, she would impose all these rules. I did not know what to make of Fabienne. She was strange, severe and cold. I never managed to touch her heart. Once, I was supposed to spend a weekend with her and her friend Julienne. Julienne's two children were there, too. The weekend was beautiful and strange at the same time. Julienne's daughter kept making racist comments, but Fabienne said I should be kind to her. That was hard for me, but I was nice to the little brat! Her elder brother was very kind and accommodating. It was hard to believe that they were siblings. That was the last weekend I spent with Fabienne.

Later, she invited me to her new home. She was in a relationship with a US soldier at the time, and that afternoon was also very strange. Their driver picked me up and took me to the house and when I got there, I saw Fabienne, who was still in bed with her boyfriend. She jumped up and put on a nightgown and came to greet me. Then she put a war film in the VCR and went back to the bedroom! I was shocked and paralyzed by the film because it was full of violence. I wanted to get rid of the horrible pictures in my head, so went out into the garden and talked to the nice driver. I was there a long time until Fabienne came out and said it was time for me to go. That was the last time I saw Fabienne in Africa.

Some years later, Frank told me that Fabienne was a gold digger. Whenever the money ran out, she started looking for the next rich man. Frank and Fabienne's life was built on sex, drugs and alcohol rather than children and family responsibilities. And everyone knew about Frank's unpredictable nature and violent outbursts.

CHAPTER 5

Church and school

The yellow dog: Who else did you spend time with?

Sophie started to take me to church every Sunday. The service started very early in the morning. We had to get up at four o'clock in the morning to get ready. I was always so tired. Sophie gave me a shower, put cream on my skin and put me in a nice dress that she had bought specially for church, and sprayed perfume on me. She did the same for herself and her two children. And then we went to church. The church was large and decorated with lots of gold, sculptures and pictures of suffering. The priest spoke in Latin, a strange language I did not understand, and I soon fell asleep. I was sure the others did not understand what he was saying either. Church lasted the whole day. Sophie would always get angry when I fell asleep. She said if I did not believe in God, then I would never be able to walk. I wanted to walk soon, but I did not know why I always fell asleep in church! My eyes used to get so heavy that it was a real struggle for me to stay awake. One day Sophie gave up and stopped taking me to church. Of course, I wanted to walk, run and jump like the others. I didn't know why God had made me sick or why he would not heal me quickly. Why did he let my parents give me up to strangers? Why did he let Fabienne abandon me? Why did he make Frank beat me and hate me? Why was I the only one of seven children to become sick? I couldn't believe in God, but how could I tell Sophie? I did not want to spoil her happiness, so I said nothing.

I sank into my thoughts and created my own adventures, like the ones in the books I had read. I dreamed of a prince who would come to save me, or that I was kidnapped by pirates and eventually managed to escape. I liked flipping through fashion magazines, because the women in the pictures looked so carefree and pretty and dressed beautifully. I started to dream that when I was older I would be a pretty woman and would be in beautiful pictures like those. I dreamed of a modeling career. I liked reading Asterix comics too. I wanted to be as strong as Obelix to defend myself against my adoptive father! When I wasn't reading or dreaming on the beach, I loved playing with my new schoolfriends and exploring our neighborhood.

My two fathers had found a private school for me: Ecole de la Vague. The headmistress was a Frenchwoman called Ivette. She was very friendly towards me and we became very close.

But the first time we went there, she wanted to know my date of birth. I remember my father and Frank looked horrified and left the room. A short time later they came back in, giggling, and took me outside. They told me to choose between 1982 and 1983. I chose 1982. Suddenly I was seven years old!

On my first day of school, I couldn't wait to see Ivette again. Frank was not there, so Ali, the man from Gaya, drove me to school. He just carried me into the classroom and left. I did not know any of the children and felt abandoned. Ivette asked the children to introduce themselves, but when it was my turn, I was afraid. My whole body started to shake because I did not know my name. Hawa Makhawa did not exist anymore. I had been rejected by my family in Gaya and my new parents had not given me a new name. I did not want to be Hawa Makhawa because it brought all the memories back. When Ivette asked me for my name, I said I didn't have one yet. Ivette said, "But you do have a name. You told me." Then I began to tremble and shouted, "That's not my name!" I crept under her table and sobbed my heart out. Ivette hugged me and calmed me down. She took me out of the classroom and asked me what had happened, and I told her everything. After that, she gave me time to get used school.

Slowly but surely, I did get used to my new school and started to talk and play with my schoolfriends and other teachers. I always liked to sink into my thoughts. I watched everything closely and thought about what I saw. The children in my class came from all over the world. We were curious about each other: Why do you look like that? Where do you come from? What happens if you stay in the sun for too long? When Ivette taught us about the continents, she told us that millions of years ago our ancestors came from Africa and crossed the Bering Strait, and that their bodies had adapted to different environmental conditions, so we developed in different ways. She told us we must never think that we are different just because we look different. We did not know anything about racial segregation in that school. And I was never excluded or treated differently because of my disability. Together, we always found a way to play, even in our annual drama show. Once the show was about Egypt and I played the part of Cleopatra's panther! I was extremely happy about that. The schoolyard was covered with sand, which made it easier for me to crawl. We had our own playground with a swing and slide. At noon we ate lunch at school and after that we had to take a nap. Ivette let me take off my leg braces at school, so I could play more easily. She never told Frank about it, because he thought I ought to wear them 24 hours a day. He could never put himself in my position. In the schoolyard, I regularly found things in the sand that people had lost. I gave them to Ivette and soon she set up a treasure chest for them in her office.

When Fabienne was still around, she had arranged for me to have a glass of milk every morning before I went to school. I hated milk! Every time I swallowed, a feeling of nausea rose up in me and I had to fight to keep it down. Afterwards, in school, I always ended up vomiting. There were arguments with Sophie every morning about this glass of milk because no one believed me when I complained of nausea.

At school we started to learn to read and write. Since I was always looking at magazines, I was familiar with the alphabet. After understanding the emphasis and the order of the words, I quickly realized that reading and writing consisted of several words strung together, and I had to put them together like a puzzle. I practiced a lot at home, and at school I spent a lot of time sitting in the book corner reading. One day Ivette came to me and wanted to know what I was doing. I said "Reading." She asked me to read her something, so I did. She looked at me in astonishment and asked where I had learned to do that. I told her that I taught myself and she praised me for it. Ivette asked if I wanted to assist her in class. I really enjoyed helping others learn the alphabet. Once I had read all the books in the classroom, Ivette gave me other books to read. I became a bookworm. I wanted to know all the words. I found a dictionary in the classroom and asked Ivette if I could take it home with me. She said I could keep it until Monday. So I spent the entire weekend with the dictionary. First, I marked all the words I already knew, and then I started to learn the unknown words. I learned the dictionary in one weekend and I felt great, although my friends were cross with me because I had no time to play, and my nanny just shook her head.

I loved school. I was often invited to other people's birthday parties and on my first birthday after I started school, Frank and Fabienne let me invite my friends over for a party too. Fabienne bathed me and gave me a nice dress to wear, although I did not feel comfortable in dresses because I was supposed to keep them clean. When my friends arrived, we ate cakes and drank tea and juice and danced. Then a clown came and made us laugh. Next came the most exciting part: my gift! Frank and Fabienne brought in a huge cardboard box. It was almost as tall as me and everyone sang happy birthday. I was supposed to blow out the candles on my cake and make a wish. Then I was allowed to unwrap my gift.

I pulled the wrapping off and saw a box. I opened the box and found another box inside, and so it went on and on, and my gift became smaller and smaller. Finally, there it was: the Barbie I wanted. I was very happy and thankful, but also a little disappointed because I thought I was going to get something very big. Later I asked Frank why my present was inside so many boxes. He told me it was a joke.

Ivette always gave me books and I read them fast. Her lessons were funny. When she turned to write on the blackboard, she always knew who was doing something stupid behind her back. It became a game where she had to guess who the culprit was. The punishment, if we were too naughty, was to spend ten minutes in a corner. If you stayed quiet, looking at the wall, she released you quickly, but if you continued to mess about, you had to stay in your corner. I think I was put in the corner once or twice.

Ivette used to take me with her in the summer vacation, so that I was not left on my own. She became my new mother. She was strict but never evil. She wanted me to carry on learning in the vacation so that I would not forget everything again, but after that I could do what I wanted. And I did. I was allowed to stay in the room belonging to her two adult daughters and play with the toys. Of course, afterwards I had to clear everything away. The two of us became inseparable. She treated me like her own daughter. Sometimes we visited her friends, or we all went to the beach together.

Ivette had fulfilled her dream of setting up a multicultural school in Africa. She was a pretty woman. She had been a ballerina when she was younger and she still looked like a dancer: straight and tall with long blond hair that hung all the way down to below her buttocks. She was married to a Togolese man and they had two girls, who were already adults. She drove a very old "beetle" car. Everyone used to laugh at her because it was always breaking down, but she did not want to get rid of it. I always wanted to go in the trunk, just for fun. With her, I was allowed to play once I'd done my homework, and I was allowed to cry like a little girl. She carried me everywhere: at the market, and even at school. She told me that I was her little baby. She would have liked to adopt me. She taught me everything: how to be polite, how to improve my reading and writing, and how to do handicrafts. She taught me things that my adoptive parents had not taught me: that work comes before play, that I should go to bed early and brush my teeth every day.

Ivette never saw Frank hit me. She knew about it because she saw the marks on Monday mornings and other people said things. If she had seen Frank raise his hand towards me, she would have called the police immediately. Frank knew that, so he was careful around her.

CHAPTER 6

Flying

The yellow dog: What about your disability. You haven't mentioned that much.

I still had to go to the hospital regularly to be examined. One day the doctors discovered that something was wrong with my left hip and recommended an operation. The operation could only be carried out in Switzerland, and an aid organization was willing to plan and pay for the trip. It was the first time I had flown anywhere and I was very excited. I could not imagine what flying would be like. I was going on my own because Frank was in Germany at that time. Sophie packed my bag the night before and called a taxi to take me to the airport. I was greeted by a lovely stewardess who had a wheelchair for me. The stewardess was there purely just to take care of me and she did not leave my side. When we finally got on the plane, my excitement soared. The stewardess calmed me down and played with me until all the passengers were in their seats.

When the plane started rolling, I turned to the window and looked out. First the plane rolled slowly and then faster and faster. The pressure of taking off forced me to lean back. I closed my eyes then and when I felt the pressure in my ears, I started to pray silently, "Please God, protect us." When I opened my eyes, we were already in the air. I opened my eyes wide and said, "Wow! I want to take off again." During the flight I was given something to eat. I watched some children's movies, slept a little and was given a gift bag by the flight crew. The flight lasted nearly ten hours but was over much too soon.

A team with a wheelchair was waiting for me at Bern Airport. I had to go on a shuttle bus to the hospital. This was where my lovely escort stewardess had to say goodbye. I did not want to let her go and I started crying, but she said, "I'll wait here and fly back with you afterwards." That calmed me down and the bus driver was finally able to set off.

I looked out of the bus window and immediately noticed that everything was clean and tidy. And there were hundreds of cars, and endless tarred roads in all directions. The houses were very different from those in Volta and Gaya. They were taller and wider and had pointed rooves and chimneys. Chimneys! I immediately remembered Santa Claus and thought, "Lucky people!"

I had never seen such green countryside. It was magical. I was fascinated by the way the fields were arranged so perfectly. Suddenly, on the left, I could see tall mountains with snow. And on the right there was an enormous, clear lake. My gaze froze. "Wow, what's that?" I asked. The driver grinned. He told me that there were quite a lot of animals like deer, hares and wolves living there. I was amazed because that meant that the fairy tales and adventures I had read were true. I felt as if I were part of a story and I fell in love with the landscape.

The journey was over too soon. At the hospital, a friendly nurse brought me to my room. Luckily, I was not alone there. My roommate was a lot older than me and she grinned when she saw me. I felt very comfortable with her. There was a huge room full of toys, and I quickly got to know other children as well. Early the next morning, the door to my room opened, and I saw Frank standing there holding lots of presents. I was very happy and we hugged each other. I truly thought that from now on everything would turn out for the best.

The doctors examined me and talked a lot to Frank as well, although I don't know what they said. Once, early in the morning, before Frank had arrived, a nurse wanted to take a blood sample. The moment I saw the needle I started screaming. My roommate tried to calm me down. She said she had done it too and nothing bad had happened to her. She said she would give me a surprise if I was brave about it. I liked her very much and trusted her, so I closed my eyes tight so that I did not have to see the needle drilling into my skin.

On the day of the operation I was very nervous and tense. A nurse dressed me a green shirt, which was completely open at the back, and some matching underwear. The day before the operation I had been told not to eat anything and they put a thick white cream on the back of my hand with a transparent plaster over it. The cream would numb my hand so that I wouldn't feel any pain when the anesthesiologist inserted the cannula. When I was wheeled into the operating theatre on a bed, I could see that some people were already there waiting. They were dressed completely in green too, and I couldn't see their faces because they wore surgical masks.

The anesthetist was very kind to me. I didn't even feel the needle. He said I should count to ten, but I only got as far as three. I remember being surrounded by deep darkness. At some point I began to hear voices in the distance, which came closer and closer. When I finally opened my eyes, there was a bright light hurting my eyes. I turned my head to the side and saw someone coming towards me and smiling. I was very confused at first because it took a while to return to full consciousness. When I did, I could feel something cool covering my body. I was in another plaster cast. But this one went all the way from my feet up to my chest, with an opening between my legs so that I could go to the toilet. The doctors had fixed my left hip with screws and I was in a lot of pain! My roommate was waiting for me when I got back to the room. She tried to distract me from the pain. Later, Frank came to visit, but after a conversation with one of the doctors, he came back scowling. Later, Frank told me that the doctor had told him that he had to beat "nigger children" to make them obey! That he should force me to exercise so that the operation would not be for nothing. And that the operation was extremely expensive, and that I should be grateful.

My roommate was discharged, and we exchanged addresses so we could keep in touch. Luckily, I was able to leave the hospital as well soon after that and was taken to another facility to recuperate. There were children from all over the world in that place – children with various war injuries and diseases. We all got on very well and the staff were very fond of me. I had to spend several weeks lying down, which was very annoying. I could only lie on my back or on my stomach and they had to push a potty under me, which I found very uncomfortable. On a lie-down wheelchair I could move around if I lay on my stomach. Frank visited me twice in that place: at the beginning of my stay and at the end. He also brought gifts for all the other children, which I thought was very nice of him. Time seemed to me to be an eternity here and I missed Ivette and my friends in Volta more and more. After some weeks, I went back to the hospital and the plaster came off. Here, I was given physiotherapy for the first time ever, and did a lot of swimming.

One day, Frank came to the hospital and brought Fabienne with him as a surprise. She stayed with me for a few hours and took me for a walk in the hospital grounds in the wheelchair. She was a stranger to me by then. I was so happy when I could leave the hospital and go back home. The lovely flight assistant was at the airport as promised and we flew back to Volta together. The return flight was not as nice as the outward flight because I could not sit up for long and was in a lot of pain, but my assistant took good care of me. I was going to see Ivette and my friends at last, after three months away. I could hardly wait to tell them about my experiences. Sadly, I had to stay at home for a while after I got back to Volta, because the pain lasted a long time. Frank was still in Germany, so Sophie took care of me. I was so glad when I was allowed to go back to school, and all my friends were pleased to see me again too.

CHAPTER 7

Waiting to leave

The yellow dog: The political situation in Volta changed, didn't it?

It was my fourth year in Volta. I made a new friend at school called Daniela. Daniela was German – one of the few pupils with pale skin, blond hair and blue eyes. She was also tall and good-looking. She did whatever she wanted. Daniela's parents had emigrated from Germany to Africa when she was a baby, so Volta was her home. By the time I met her, her parents were already separated. Her mother, Petra, quickly made friends with Frank and everyone could see she had a crush on him.

I was allowed to spend as much time with Daniela as I wanted. She didn't like Frank either, but she was not afraid of him and was always defending me because she did not like the way he treated me. Daniela was very upset when her parents separated because she loved her father more than anything and wanted to be with him all the time. For a while, we used to spend weekends at her father's house outside Volta. Her two best friends would come too. The four of us always had fun and we were allowed to do what we wanted there. Daniela's father trusted her and there were no rules. We ate when we wanted, slept when we wanted, went wherever we wanted. And we were sensible because we did not want to endanger our freedom.

Overnight, the mood in Togo changed. Something bad was in the air. Early one morning, I woke up to hear a huge noise from a loudspeaker and shouting outside. I quickly got dressed and went out. Everybody was standing outside, and I asked Sophie what was happening. She told me the police had caught a thief and had tied him to a truck by his hands. Every few minutes they would hammer a nail into his head. The same information came over the loudspeakers. The president's army was driving the man round all the neighborhoods to show everyone what happened to thieves. I could not believe it at first and waited for the loudspeakers to come closer. Then I saw the truck with the man tied to it and saw them slowly hammering a nail into his head! I only looked briefly but I could see the blood running from his head. Then I hid behind Sophie. I tried very hard after that to get those pictures out of my head. How could the president allow people to be so cruel to each other? Soon we were all living in fear. The president was more unpredictable and evil than Frank and could strike anyone at any time. Soon there were soldiers, tanks and corpses all over the street.

Everyone who could get away left. All the foreigners had gone or were preparing to leave. The school was closed. Ivette had already left the country with her family. She wanted to take me with her, but Frank did not want her to. My neighborhood friends were gone too and I understood why. I lived with Sophie and her family for a while, but soon they also had to leave, before it was too late.

For the last few months, before Daniela and I left for Germany, we lived with a friend of her mother's. Daniela's mom told me that Frank was in Germany arranging papers for me so I could leave. The villa Daniela and I stayed in during those last few months was huge. We felt like princesses. There was a maid, a gardener, a cook and a housekeeper. There was also a pool and we spent every day there because we weren't allowed to leave the house. We would swim and lie in the sun, then the cook would serve us food and after dinner we would go inside to play or read.

We didn't want to go to Germany because we knew that everything would be different there. On the map we could see that there was no sea near the place we were going to. How were we supposed to live without the sea? And the idea that we would have to speak

German also upset us. The language sounded hard and cold to us. We tried to comfort ourselves with the thought that we would return to Volta after the war.

CHAPTER 8

Germany

The yellow dog: What was it like living in Germany with Frank?

The day Daniela and I had to leave Togo we were very, very sad. We were also afraid because we knew that I would be living on my own with Frank! I had a premonition that a long gloomy time was about to begin. My tummy felt weird, although I wasn't sick.

I was not excited about this flight because I had already flown twice before. This time I was only concerned with my anxiety about the uncertainty ahead. I was afraid of living with Frank. For Daniela, flying was almost normal, and she was going to stay with her dear grandma. Her mother would follow later. The flight was also the last time we would be together for a while.

We had a very nice flight attendant called Laura who took care of us. She was particularly fond of me, but Daniela was annoyed because she thought Laura was being nice to me out of pity. Laura and I exchanged addresses and she became one of the most important people in my life later on.

When we arrived at the airport in Germany, Daniela and I had to separate. I was picked up by Frank and I could not judge his mood, so I assumed the worst. But he was kind to me. He had brought a long pair of pants, a sweater and a winter jacket for me because it was already winter in Germany. He pulled the warm clothes on me, took the luggage and we went to the car. I was walking with my leg braces and crutches. He showed me the surroundings and took me into the woods, where I walked on snow for the first time. I did not like it! Everything was so new to me, especially the steam that came out of my mouth.

From the woods, we drove to Frank's parents' house. We drove past meadows, fields, mountains and forests. The landscape immediately reminded me of the Grimms' fairy tales and of Hansel and Gretel, who were lost in the forest.

I had never seen so many signs and traffic lights. Frank stopped at every red light, although there was often no other vehicle in front of him. I found this strange, because in Volta people drove through most of the red lights. Frank wanted me to buckle up in the car and told me that I had to do this every time or there would be trouble with the police. In Volta, you never had to wear a seat belt. Everything looked so different. The first thing that caught my eye was how clean and tidy everything was. The place was even cleaner than Switzerland!

I did not know Frank's parents and had no idea whether they would receive me warmly. When we arrived, I was greeted very kindly by his mother. She even hugged me, brought me tea and made me some bread and jam. Frank's father was less friendly. He looked at me crossly and muttered to himself. I did not understand what he was saying because I only spoke French, but whatever it was, it did not sound nice to me.

Gradually, I got to know the entire family, which was large. Frank was one of seven siblings and almost all of them were married with children. The family welcomed me, and I soon got on well with my cousins, uncles and aunts.

Frank's home, when we got there, turned out to be the smallest, oldest house in the neighborhood and it was very crooked. It was hard to see how it could still be standing! I went inside and found it very cozy and warm. I had my own room on the ground floor and Frank slept upstairs. Downstairs there was a spacious living room, which was half full of his monkey bikes. Monkey bikes are very small motorcycles and they were Frank‘s greatest passion. The kitchen, bathroom and a guest room were also on the ground floor. Under the house there was a cellar – something I had never come across in Mali or Togo. I only had a little bag and a few books to unpack. I hoped that the container with all my toys and gifts would arrive soon.

The next day, we went to visit Frank's sister Sylvia. I already knew about her from Frank's tales and was very anxious to meet her at last. I knew Frank loved her because he had shown me lots of pictures of her and her boys. Sylvia was tall with curly blond hair and blue eyes, like Frank. She looked very well cared for and smelled nice. Their house was much larger than Frank's and very clean and tidy. They even had a nice garden. Sylvia was married and had three sons, with whom I got on very well. I immediately took to Sylvia and I was very glad she was there. Sylvia regularly cleaned Frank´s house for him and he always brought me to see her when I wanted him to. I quickly learned to trust her, and she taught me how to cook and bake. Sylvia became an important point of reference for me.

Frank made great efforts at first. He showed me many beautiful places and introduced me to his friends and acquaintances – something I was not expecting. He always told people proudly about what he had done for me or was still doing for me. In the first year, I often travelled with him to visit his family.

I remember the first time I went to the outdoor swimming pool with them. Even at the desk, people looked at me strangely. I wore skirts at that time, which were more practical with the leg braces, and people were staring at my legs. That hurt me a lot because no one had done that to me before. It seemed as if no one had anything better to do than stare at me! They watched every single movement as I took off my leg braces and as I crawled to the water. Once I was in the water, they did not watch me as much because they could not see my thin legs, but when I got out again, everyone started staring again! Lots of children came up to me and said, "Wow, you have thin legs" and pointed at them. They laughed too and that hurt. I started to hide my legs under the towel. My uncle and aunts tried to reassure me, and one of my older cousins defended me.

At that time, I couldn't speak German but I was able to interpret very well what people wanted. Frank also translated. I soon realized that I was different and that some people had a problem with it. If they weren't staring at me because of my disability, they were staring because of my skin color! Things were exactly the same on the street. People stared at me all the time and I often fell over because I did not know how to handle it. I felt like a circus attraction! Why did they behave like that? Where was their sense of decency? In Africa, people never stared at my legs. They helped me, or they prayed for me.

The staring followed me for years. People would ask why I was black and whether I knew what a television was. Most of them thought that people in Africa were wild animals. Wherever I went, I was the only dark-skinned, disabled girl. Frank's father was ashamed of me because of my dark skin and disability. To most of Frank's siblings and the local people, I was the "nigger child," although I was too young at the time to know that this was a pejorative label.

Every night for a year, I waited at the window for people come out onto the street, but they never did. I wondered why everyone went home in the evening instead of meeting outside, even if it was just on the doorstep. The only noises I could hear came from the vehicles driving past. I missed Africa! There, everyone, whether poor or rich, always chatted on the street, especially in the evening when the sun went down. People would sit together to talk and laugh and they would dance. The soundscape in Volta was always noisy. Even at night you could hear the crickets chirping, owls hooting, dogs howling and other kinds of noises. In Africa, people are never alone because the doors are always open. I could go to anyone's house at any time and stay there. I never had to make an appointment in advance to see anyone. It was all so different in Germany. Even the food did not taste nice to me. The vegetables and meat were so bland.

I started learning German very quickly. I sucked up words like a sponge. If I didn't understand something, I asked Sylvia or Frank and I always got an explanation. I quickly understood the correlations and then I started practicing reading and writing. I asked Frank how to pronounce ö, ü, ä and ß and he taught me the sounds. I wrote words down to see and feel the spelling, then I played guessing games where I thought of a word in French and tried writing the German equivalent. Then I looked in the dictionary. I quickly learned to read because I wanted to read books and I already knew my few French books by heart. It was very difficult to get hold of French books in Germany. Unfortunately, the container from Africa never arrived. All my childhood memories from my homeland were gone. I still mourn those things.

I practiced diligently and was soon able to write and understand German, but I was not ready to speak it yet. With Frank, I spoke French as usual but I was curious to know what he and the others said about me. I listened closely to their conversations, especially when they started talking about me. That was how I discovered that he said bad things about me to his family and friends. He would say things like: "What am I supposed to do with this disabled nigger child?" or "She just sits there, playing and doing nothing!" or "Lazybones!" or "She should be grateful to me. Without me she would still be wallowing in filth!" and "Even her parents did not want her anymore, that's why they sold her to me!" (For a long time, I thought this was just another way of humiliating me but, sadly, I discovered later that it was a true story.) He also said, "Why is she ruining my life?" He seemed to forget that I never wanted to live with him. I felt as rejected by him as by my mother in Gaya.

CHAPTER 9

Beatings

The yellow dog: Was that the start of the dark era?

Frank changed again all of a sudden. He started forbidding me from doing things, he yelled at me and went back to hitting and threatening me. He would raise his arms and clench one hand into a fist. His face would be red and sometimes he even foamed at the mouth, like a dog with rabies! I saw a dog like that in Volta once. But when he puckered his lips like a fish, I knew it was too late.

Frank started making me exercise every day on my own. He said I had to if I wanted to walk again. I had to start cleaning the house and he gave me chores to do. He wanted me to learn to do the shopping on my own, and to work so that I could support my family in Africa. He said I had a very good life in Germany. He was not interested in the fact that I was only eleven years old and still had a lot to learn.

Frank forced me to wear my leg braces every day because I could not crawl around Germany the way I did in Africa. I walked like a robot and it was very tiring. The longer I walked, the weaker my body became. The braces had been made in Togo and looked awful. They were heavy and constricting. The corset crushed my rib cage so that I could barely breathe and it was constantly pinching me. Walking with it was so exhausting that every little step made me sweat. My arms quickly began to tremble because they had to support and hold my entire weight. The orthopedist eventually found that my right shoulder had also been affected by polio. The ball of my shoulder joint was located some way below the socket, with only a thin strand of muscle connecting my arm to my shoulder.

I was so relieved to get my first set of German leg braces, and very happy when the orthopedist decided to leave off the corset. Now I could be flexible. The new leg braces were modern and made from carbon and had flexible knee joints. If I wanted to sit down, I could bend my knees by pulling on a long transparent cord that connected my thighs to my knees. To stand up, I had to snap the straps in place first to hold my legs stiff. But the straps kept coming undone while I was walking, and I kept falling down. The orthopedist had to change my leg braces every year because I was growing. The doctors also started questioning my diagnosis because they said it was unusual for kids with polio to grow so fast.

We kept having to go to the youth welfare office because my residence status had not yet been settled. Frank always told me to be nice to the woman there and not tell her anything if I wanted to stay in Germany. I didn't want to stay in Germany, but where else could I go, when even my parents did not want me? While Frank and the woman talked, I would paint a picture to give the woman. I did not understand why she was helping my enemy and pushing for the adoption to be granted under German law. The problem was that certain conditions had to be met to adopt a child under German law and Frank did not meet any of them! But then, I had already been "adopted" in the African way without official documents and I hadn't lived with my family for a long time.

I sometimes thought I should tell the woman the truth, so she could help me. Eventually, I plucked up the courage to explain the situation at home using two dolls. The woman quickly understood what I was telling her and was horrified. She talked to Frank, who said I had invented the story because I was cross with him for not giving me what I wanted! He looked at me angrily. I knew that look and I began to tremble. The woman asked me in front Frank whether it was true that he beat me, and I said no, because I felt intimidated. In the end, Frank got all the documents he needed, and my adoption was official.

CHAPTER 10

Friends

The yellow dog: Did you go to school in Germany?

About a year after my arrival in Germany, I was allowed to go to school. I liked school very much because people were friendly. I made friends quickly and all the teachers liked me and treated me kindly. Sometimes a couple of teachers, who did not live far from me, would pick me up in the morning and drive me home again in the afternoon, which was very sweet of them. As time went on, I was often cared for by teachers or classmates and I was regularly invited to have lunch with them.

I was happy as long as I was not with Frank. I did not tell people at school about my worries and problems, but everyone realized something was not right. I was basically unresponsive until break time while I processed the blows I had received before school. After break, I rejoined the world of the living and could have fun. School became my sanctuary.

Tanja, a girl in my class, used to carry my heavy backpack so that I could climb the stairs. I hated going upstairs because it was so strenuous, and I was always drenched in sweat by the time I reached the top. Once, I had to go into hospital so the doctors could remove the screws in my hip. When I came back to school, my class organized a party to welcome me and gave me beautiful handmade cards.

By now, I could read, write and speak a little German, even though I didn't have extra German classes, so I could follow my lessons. If I said something wrong, people would correct me, and I was always thankful because I wanted to learn to speak this new language very well. My dictation was poor though, because I could never hear whether a word was written with a capital letter or not. The German teacher warned me that it would take a while to get used to the complex German grammar and spelling. About a year later, someone in the administration noticed that I had not completed an integration course – a special German language course for foreigners. Although my German was very good by then, because of bureaucracy, I had to take the course in addition to my normal lessons. Luckily, my class teacher was a teacher on this course and asked if I would like to help her, which I did gladly. I already knew everything that was taught there.

This was where I met my friend Anastasia. She came from Russia and had long, blond hair, big blue eyes, sensual red lips, a beautiful face and plenty of charisma. She was not very tall, but she had a very feminine, attractive figure and all the boys liked her. She always dressed sexily and her makeup was perfect. Anastasia was the opposite of me. She even had a boyfriend who was in her class and lived near her. For some reason, Frank hated Anastasia. If he saw us together, he would get angry and insult her. Once, Anastasia and I went to the gym together. I was worried because I knew that if Frank saw her, he would freak out again, but Anastasia was not afraid of him. She said if he did anything to me, she would go to the police immediately! Frank arrived while we were at the gym. When he saw Anastasia, he turned bright red and puckered his lips like a fish. He called her a whore and chucked her out. No one did anything and I was ashamed.

Anastasia stayed friends with me and we began to meet in secret. We got on very well, and her family and boyfriend were nice to me too. Her mother liked it when I went around there and always cooked delicious Russian specialties, like pelmeni (small Russian dumplings) in vegetable broth. I loved this soup. Anastasia's mother had polio, so she understood me very well.

I was still in contact with Ivette, my teacher from Togo. She was living in France now and we wrote letters to each other. She was like a mother to me and I missed her so much! I wanted to go to her, but I didn't know how. Then Ivette was taken seriously ill. She had cancer. In her last letter she told me that if she did not write again, it would be because she had closed her eyes forever. My heart broke in two when I stopped hearing from her. Days, weeks, months and years passed without a letter from her. I was all alone with my pain and grief. I cried in my bed every night. I used to bite the pillow so I wouldn't scream. Somehow, I seemed to lose all the lovely people around me. Although I was thankful when people took me into their hearts and gave me so much love, I saw life as unfair. I thought I must be bad, or these things would not happen to me. I prayed that Ivette's soul would rest in peace and hoped to be like her one day.

Laura, the flight attendant I met the day I left Togo, also used to send me letters and packages from all the countries she visited. Getting a package with a nice letter on my birthday or at Christmas was wonderful. We wrote lots of letters to each other and met up two or three times. She took me to the circus once and she would bathe me gently and read me nice stories until I fell asleep. Like Ivette, Laura would have liked to adopt me, but Frank banned me from seeing her again.

CHAPTER 11

Rock bottom

The yellow dog: Couldn't anyone help you?

Day-to-day life with Frank was hell. My body hurt and I had a constant headache because he kept hitting me on the head. After every blow I would see stars! The headaches also made me vomit, often suddenly. He was constantly beating me and his attacks were unpredictable.

Here is an excerpt from my diary:

> *„Today he came from work and asked me whether I had done the shopping. I told him that Silvio, his friend, was doing the shopping. He started yelling and scolding. He took his belt and was about to beat me with it but managed to control himself. But then he dropped a 10 kg parcel on my head and kicked my head too. It hurt very, very badly. He said he is not going to take care of me anymore and that he is going to tell everyone that I am a bad person and ungrateful. I don't give a shit! I want to die. No one needs me here anyway, but if this goes on then I really will kill myself!"*

Frank's attacks were getting worse year after year. He always apologized after beating me and said he did not know why he did it. I believed him. On the one hand, I could feel his positive intentions and on the other, I could feel he had a tremendous hatred and resentment towards me. I was thankful that, because of him, I had a roof over my head and medical care and that I was living better than my family in Africa. But I could not understand why I was treated like a worthless animal – by him, by Fabienne, who was no longer there, and by my biological parents.

The only news I had of my biological parents came through Frank. He informed me whenever my mother gave birth to another child. There were nine of us now, including me. I could not remember the last time I had seen my family. I did not want anything to do with my parents anymore, since I was now sure that they didn't want anything to do with me. But I missed my siblings and Niara very much and I cried myself to sleep every night.

I missed Volta terribly too. I had been away so long that I had even forgotten how to speak Mina, the Togolese language.

One day, Fabienne arrived without warning. Frank wasn't happy about it, but I was very pleased because she had always seemed elusive to me. Fabienne told me that she was going to get married soon and wanted to take me with her to become a part of her new family. She said that her future husband, a wealthy American, knew about me and liked the idea too. They wanted to start a new life in Trinidad and Tobago. I wanted to leave with her immediately to escape the beatings. Besides, I thought even if she left me on my own there, I would at least be in a more beautiful country! She shared my bed with me and it felt so good to be hugged again. She only stayed for a few days. When she left, she gave me a business card with her phone number on it. She said I should wait three days and then call her there. I was full of hope. Three days later, I called her, and a man answered. He said he would have to check the guest list because it was a hotel, and I should phone back in a bit. When I called again, he said they had left a long time ago. I was deeply disappointed. Why did Fabienne lie to me and make such promises? Frank told me that she had only come to buy herself out of the adoption arrangement with DM 10,000 and he had refused and chucked her out! There are no words to describe my disappointment. I no longer felt like a human. I felt like an object. In a way I was pleased that Frank was still looking after me and that he never abandoned me or lied to me.

The only person I still trusted and felt affection for was Sylvia, Frank's sister. She helped me whenever she could. But the more she did for me, the more aggressive he became towards her. He started threatening her too, so I stopped talking to Sylvia about Frank and decided not to see her as often as I used to. Sylvia had a very kind old neighbor. Even before I met her, when I was still living in Volta, this neighbor had made me a pair of pants that I could wear more easily over my leg braces. She sewed a long zipper down the entire length of the pants. Whenever I went to see Sylvia, I also visited her neighbor. We would drink tea, eat cakes and chat. I was incredibly thankful to this lovely old lady because she saw me as a person.

I also used to visit an old lady who lived opposite Frank's mother. She always beamed all over her face when she saw me through the window, and she would ask me to come up. She was good to me. She offered me tea and cake and when I left, she always gave me candy or money. Frank knew this and said I should save the money for my family, because they did not have enough to eat, and I was well off in Germany. I never understood why I should give the money to my non-existent African family that had given me away, so I saved it for myself.

One day, Frank asked for the money and I did not have it anymore. I had bought a pair of sunglasses with my savings. I told him it was my money and that I had bought something with it. He was furious and beat me, shouting that I was a heartless thief. Afterwards he apologized again, but that kind of treatment cannot simply be excused, and certainly not when it has become a daily occurrence. He always found reasons to beat me. I was at my wits' end because no matter what I did or didn't do, the violence kept getting worse.

I felt nothing anymore. I craved death and peace. About this time, I read in a teenage magazine about a girl who regularly cut herself. She said the physical pain blocked out the emotional pain and it made her feel free. I wanted to know if that was true. Would I really suffer less if I cut myself? I tried it, and it was true – I managed to distract myself a bit and focus my attention on something else. At the same time, it was a kind of introduction because my goal was to slit my wrists. When I was thirteen, all I thought about was dying. The only question was: How?

A short time later, Frank hit me again. That was the last straw. I waited until I was alone, then I wrote a farewell letter. I planned to cut my wrists but found I could not. As the blade reached my vein, I felt a deep, dull pain and suddenly I did not want to do it this way anymore. I smeared the blood on the letter and went out of my room. I collected all the old medicines from Frank‘s drug bag, took a bottle of vodka and then went back to my room. I swallowed a lot of pills and then drank diligently. I had never drunk alcohol before, but I did not care. I fell asleep in a fog. Afterwards, it seemed to me that something left my body. Everything around me was pitch black. I do not know how long I was gone.

At some point I regained consciousness and wondered where I was. Darkness was everywhere around me. I panicked and called out. Suddenly, two beings in black robes appeared. One of them was holding a huge brown book in his hands. They linked arms on either side of me and said, "Come on, we have something to show you." We flew through the clouds and they seemed to be in a hurry. We stopped and a black cloud opened before us. We looked down and saw the rain dripping down. There was something sad about the rain and I wanted to go down there to look at it more closely. Then one of the beings said to me, "Stay calm" and "Look what's happening now. Remember that!" I overcame my fear and looked. I saw lots of black umbrellas moving about. After a while, the crowd dissolved a little. The rain eased, and the umbrellas were folded up. Now I could see the faces. I saw some people I knew, but they were very, very sad. I heard them saying, "Why didn't she come to me? I would have helped her!" Another said, "I never noticed anything was wrong. Why did she do it?" I asked the beings who the people were talking about. "Look there," they said, and I saw a grave in front of me. I felt something strange in my belly and when I looked at the tombstone, I saw my name was engraved on it. "Oh, no!" I cried. "What have I done?" I told the two beings that I was sorry for what I had done, that I did not realize what the consequences would be, and never thought that people would grieve for me. I promised them that I would never try to kill myself again, no matter what I went through in this life. I begged them to give me another chance.

Suddenly, I heard a ringing that kept getting louder and louder. Slowly, I opened my eyes. It was my alarm clock. I turned it off and wondered. My eyes were wide open, and I was somehow clear and empty at the same time. I began to tidy up. I burned my farewell letter, cleared the tablets and bottle away, took a shower, got dressed, grabbed my backpack and went to the bus stop.

I was way too early, but I didn't mind. I waited. It was winter, and I enjoyed the cold wind. I could not really think about anything yet. I was just there, and I felt very well, physically. It was as if I was truly seeing everything for the first time, and in me there was such a silence. I felt one with something higher than myself. I was sure I had not set my alarm clock, and why would I plan to get up at four o'clock in the morning anyway? I always set my alarm for five o'clock. I didn't mention it to anyone and nobody noticed anything different. Only I realized that something had changed inside me. One thing was clear: No matter what I experienced in my life from then on, I would never do such a thing again. I was also aware that I had a task to perform before I could leave this planet. I couldn't tell exactly what my task would be, but a new force was born inside me that night and I knew I was protected. I understood that there is a greater power above us and it wants to help and protect us.

Still, the violence continued every day and I could not bear it anymore. I wondered if I was ungrateful. After all, Frank made sure I had enough to eat, and I was able to go to school and live in Europe. What more did I want? Maybe I deserved the beatings. Maybe I wasn't supposed to be happy. I hadn't laughed in ages. I wondered what my future would look like. Would I ever have a boyfriend? Children? I prayed and dreamed of a life without violence and, somehow, I found a deep trust in life and a confidence within me. I could hear a soft voice whispering that this would soon pass. I knew I was not as heartless as my mothers. I could never treat a child the way they had, especially not if that child was sick. Children need to be cared for and loved.

One day, I thought again about the woman from the youth welfare office. Maybe she could help me. By now I was a bit older and my German was much better. I phoned the woman and told her what Frank was doing to me. She came over and immediately asked Frank, who was standing next to me, whether what I had told her on the phone was true. Of course, he denied it. He said, "You know what children are like. It was just a harmless slap." The woman looked at me crossly and left. Do these people really believe that an offender will admit his guilt immediately when asked? And why would a child make up something that awful? This incident with the youth welfare office made everything worse. Their job is to protect children, but in reality, they leave children in the lurch because they trust the parents more.

Since Frank threatened anyone who liked me and wanted to help me, I could not go to any of these people. Suicide was no longer an option either, but I did not want any more violence. I was so very tired! I began to think about running away and living on the street.

CHAPTER 12

Back to Africa

The yellow dog: Did you ever see your family in Africa again?

Frank took me to Africa twice. He had a thirst for adventure and told my head teacher that the trip was important for me because my birth family lived there. The head teacher made an exception and let me take three months off school if I promised to catch up on everything I missed.

We drove from Germany to Mali. Frank knew the route and planned everything meticulously. He packed lots of tools and car parts in case we broke down, and a lot of beer to bribe customs officers. Over time, Frank had become an expert on Africa. It was clear to everyone that he knew exactly what he was doing and that everything would go well. Luckily, there were always other people in the car with us.

On the first trip he took his "dropout" buddies along. I knew the guys and liked them all, especially Joe and Harri. Joe was small and slender and half bald. His car was called Mausi. He was very funny, especially when he was drunk. Harri was tall with long dark-blond hair and a very long beard. He was a man with a heart and a soul – a rocker and a Harley Davidson fan. Despite his appearance, he was a lovely, sensitive man.

I was very excited about the trip, because I was going to Africa at last – for the first time since leaving Gaya. I took along gifts for everyone. The journey was extremely beautiful, educational and interesting. We drove through many different countries and slept in the car or in the open. First, we passed through France, where I particularly admired the Pyrenees, a mountain range stretching from the Mediterranean to the Atlantic. There were delightful mountain passes everywhere and the landscape was beautiful. It changed as we neared Spain, but the people in both countries seemed to take life at a more relaxed pace. I liked Spain very much. I loved the cultural influence of the Arabs, who conquered the country in the Middle Ages. The Alhambra, in Granada, is a particularly fine example of their influence. It is a palatial complex made up of palaces that are predominantly decorated with wood and mosaic elements. Everywhere you look, there is beautiful decoration, with arabesques and muqarnas on ceilings and walls that make you dream. My favorite food there was tortilla. While the boys were enjoying the nightlife in Granada, I tried to sleep in the car, but I found it difficult because I was afraid of being kidnapped.

After a few days, we reached the border town of Ceuta, a Spanish city on the North African coast of the Strait of Gibraltar, a strait that connects the Mediterranean Sea with the Atlantic Ocean. Luckily, we did not stop there for long. I did not like Ceuta, because danger lurked everywhere. The military was very, very strict and checked all our documents several times before they would let us onto the ferry. When we reached the other side I breathed a sigh of relief! In Morocco I felt at home. It was clear I had arrived on the black continent: Tangier, Rabat, Casablanca, Marrakesh and then across to Agadir and Dakhla. The people of Morocco seemed very friendly. I was often invited to dinner and always received gifts and prayers along the way. Of course, Frank bullied me! Everyone who said a word to help me immediately became his enemy.

Everyone who wanted to cross the desert met at a campsite in Dakhla. When enough travelers had gathered, they drove off in a convoy because the route was mined. The military was also very strict and checked everyone's documents carefully, so we never left on time.

Once we reached the gateway to the desert, we knew that from then on, the trip was purely about survival.

The journey across the Sahara Desert was unique. The desert filled me. I always felt an amazing sense of inner peace in the desert. And there was a harmony in the group that was not there before and did not last after we left the desert. Frank and I got on very well. There was no violence and no more stupid proverbs. Now was the time for teamwork. Before we set off into the desert we packed a lot of water and food – enough to survive. We were told not to get out of the car, not to get lost and, more importantly, not to leave the group. There were no more power games. This was not our territory. The desert was in charge!

It is landscape enveloped in an invisible, positive force and if intruders respect it and appreciate it, they can pass through unharmed. Origin, religion and faith do not matter in the desert. Our only reliable sources were the sun, the wind and the sea. The sun also determined our time window for travelling because we drove from when it rose in the east to when it set in the west. The wind also let us identify the points of the compass and told us how far we were from the sea. Death was omnipresent in the desert. The landscape evoked a sense of awe, strength, love and perfection. I always knew that, no matter how long we were there, everything would turn out well. An inner voice told me that as long as I trusted life, I would reach the other side. I learned from the desert that the world is more than what I see, that the universe is so omnipotent that I can never fully grasp it with my human mind. It goes on and on, with no end in sight. I loved sleeping under the gigantic roof of stars. I was not afraid anymore, because I was guarded and protected.

I loved it when a sandstorm blew up. You could hear the wind whistle, the sky was obliterated with sand and a sudden darkness arose. For protection, we either stayed in the car or on the ground covered with a blanket, and waited quietly until it passed over. The wind whistled a beautiful melody, the sweet melody of life. When the storm was over, there was sand everywhere.

Our next destination was Nouakchott in Mauritania. It is a very strict country, but the coastal route to Senegal was gorgeous. When we reached Senegal we felt free. It was time to relax. I enjoyed eating fresh fish there, and I found the fishermen's children fascinating. They all had beautiful skin and blond hair that had been bleached by the saltwater and sun. The fishermen seemed to dominate the sea, although most of them could not swim. I felt their respect for the sea. They seemed to know every wave, and it occurred to me that they were observing the waves and testing the wind before they set out on their pirogues. These are fishing boats made of wood that are propelled through the water using a long pole. In Senegal you could feel people's zest for life. They seemed to me to be much happier and somehow freer.

In Dakar, the group separated. The others were keen to see the Gambia, while I went on alone with Frank to Mali. I was looking forward to seeing my siblings and friends and my dear Aunt Niara.

Mali is a very beautiful country and I enjoyed the trip from south to north. I found it amazing how much the vegetation changed – from lush green to a sandy wasteland.

When we arrived in Gaya, everyone recognized me immediately and started cheering and shouting, "Hawa-Khawa is here!" My siblings, friends and Niara were very happy. We were finally together again after so many years of separation. I could hardly believe it. My father, too, rejoiced very much. He hugged me tightly and his face shone. My mother was very reserved as always. Her hug was very cold. We could not talk to each other because she did not speak French and I had forgotten my mother tongue. Besides, we had nothing to say to each other. I spent time with my siblings, Aunt Niara and friends. I finally got to meet the twins and my little sister Lamina and we loved each other immediately. My little sister was always beaming and did not leave my side for a second. She made me so happy and became a source of strength to me. Of course, I loved everyone else too, but the connection with her was now the strongest. I still found security in Niara's arms and she gave me courage, because she knew exactly what I had been through and what had been done to me. She was a clairvoyant and she told me my future, but unfortunately I forgot what she said. I was overwhelmed by the whole situation.

After the initial euphoria I was puzzled and did not really understand why I was there. Kouami, who by now was a grown man, had to work a lot and was kept very busy by Frank and our father so he didn't have any time for me. If my younger siblings and Niara had not been there, I would have preferred to leave again. When I left, my younger siblings gave me lots of little gifts. It was very painful for me to leave them again and I cried in the car until I fell asleep. The pain of loss was so severe that I was tempted to forget my family.

When we arrived in Bamako, Frank sold the car and we used the money to fly back to Germany.

CHAPTER 13

Crawling

The yellow dog: What about your second trip to Gaya?

The second time I visited my family with Frank was about two years later, when I was fifteen. I was cheerful and deeply sad too. I didn't know what to make of these visits and I constantly had to suppress my sad feelings. This time, we travelled with some people I did not know very well. There was a single woman who had just started a relationship with Frank. She was very nice to me during the trip and we became friends. Over time, she saw how Frank talked about me and treated me and she became sad and cross, but the more she defended me, the more he turned against her. At some point, she left the group to travel with other people. I could understand her decision and wished I could go with her!

From then on, the journey was hell. The mood between Frank and me became increasingly menacing. When we were a day's journey from Gaya, everything slowly fell apart. I had kept one clean pair of pants for when we arrived, and he poured liquid on them. I was angry and yelled at him. I did not understand why he would do that. He stopped the car at the side of the road and hit me, shouting, "How dare you talk to me like that!" and "Is that the way you repay me for everything I've done for you?" I said that this time I would stay with my family forever and he would soon be rid of me for good.

Frank continued to beat me. Then he took my passport away and threw me out of the car. I did not have my leg braces, so I started to crawl. I was no longer accustomed to crawling and the sandy ground hurt my knees and feet. I managed to crawl as far as the street, where I hoped to catch a bus. But when a bus came past, it didn't stop and it was clear that there would not be another one for a long time. I was somewhere in the bush in the middle of Mali! After a while, Frank threw out my leg braces and told me I could keep them. Then he went back to the car. I pulled the braces on and, even though I knew that I could never reach Gaya alone, I walked away. I didn't care. If I was going to die, then so be it. Walking was very difficult because my body hurt after the beating. I was exhausted but I forced myself to keep going.

I walked a little and then stopped. I closed my eyes because they had become too heavy and I fell asleep on my feet! I woke up before I fell over and carried on. From time to time, I heard a car in the distance and I knew it must be Frank. I hid behind a bush and when the car drove past I could see that it really was him. I just thought, "Let him look for me!" What would he do if he never found me again? How would he explain it?

By now, it had become very dark. I lost all sense of time. I saw a fire burning in the distance and went over to it. A man was sitting there alone. I was worried, but I had to lie down for a moment to rest, just for a short while, so I went up to him. The man could not speak, which was a bit weird. I signaled with my hands to ask him if I could sit down. He gave me tea to drink and I asked him, with hands, whether I could lie down for a moment. He agreed and prepared a sleeping place for me.

Something told me to be very careful, but suddenly I had to vomit and then I lay down. I knew I must not really fall asleep, but my eyes were too heavy to stop them. Suddenly I felt that the man was lying next to me. He started to grope me! I sat up and said loudly, "No!" and he backed off. I lay down again. He started again, this time more aggressively and I pushed him away from me. I got up. I have never jumped up as fast as I did that time. I insulted him and walked off. Thank God he did not come after me! I walked away and at some point, I stopped and stood on the street and tried to sleep while standing up, which worked for a bit. I was aware that I was being protected by someone. Maybe it was Ivette?

The sun was slowly rising, the birds chirping. I watched a shepherd driving his flock, and then I heard a car. I knew it was Frank. This time I just thought, "Come on, get back in so you can get to Gaya safely." I stood on the street and when he saw me, he stopped, and I got back in. We did not speak at first. Later he said he'd been worried about me. I did not speak to him for the entire journey. I planned to talk to my family about what had happened. I thought they would understand. For me one thing was clear: If Frank laid a finger on me again, I would run away, no matter where!

When I reached my family, I had a black eye, a burst lip and a swollen face. Everyone knew immediately what had happened. To start with, I said I had fallen over, but nobody believed me. Frank carried on bullying me there too! He wanted me to study for school and do my exercises. I was studying, but he wanted me to study and do exercises around the clock.

The day before we left, I spoke to my mother. My brother Kouami translated for us. I told her everything. I said I could not bear to be treated like that and asked if she had a place for me. She said I should be grateful to Frank and told me to wait until I was eighteen and then I could leave because I would be of legal age. I was only fifteen, so she expected me to endure another three years of violence! Kouami and I were horrified. Was this how a loving mother behaves? I was begging to come back home, and my mother rejected me again. It was clear that I no longer belonged. But I wanted to be strong for my little siblings. They needed me, and I needed them. There was an invisible bond between us. We did not have to talk to know what was going on. And we hoped that one day we could be together. Frank was amazed when I got in the car to go back.

On the way back, Frank and I drove through Volta, but the place did not interest me anymore because I no longer knew anyone there. Not even my beloved sea could restore me then. I was empty inside, like a dead person. I could not think one clear thought. The whole journey and everything I had experienced seemed to me to be an illusion.

Back in Germany, I distributed gifts to my friends and told them only about the beautiful moments with my siblings and about all the foreigners I had met on the way.

CHAPTER 14

Betrayal

The yellow dog: Did you ever ask for help in Germany?

Every year on my birthday Frank promised me there would be no more beatings from now on.

I was so tired. I could not understand what he meant. I was alive and dead at the same time. Africa was my homeland but I could not and would not live there. In Germany no one could help me. Where could I go? Where did I belong? Who was I?

I went to school every day, went shopping, cooked and cleaned. I was always looking for distractions, but nothing helped, nothing could make me happy. The black hole in my heart was getting bigger and bigger. I became restless, could no longer concentrate. If I tried to read, I would fall asleep immediately and forget the sentences I had just read.

In the summer, I felt physically fit because I was in my element in the heat and I could go out a lot. In the autumn, the sadness slowly came on because winter was near. The winter was a nightmare for me. It was always dark and wet, and the cold entered my body no matter what I wore. I wanted to be like an animal, plant or tree and prepare myself for hibernation, and simply sleep till spring.

The longer I lived here, the harder I found it. I felt as if I was locked up in a prison. In the winter, walking was a torment because little stones were always catching on the rubber stoppers on the end of my crutches. As soon as I was on smooth ground, like at school, they just slipped out from under me and I fell down. I could not walk in snow either, but I still had to do everything on my own. My school satchel became heavier and heavier each year. I found it very difficult to climb the stairs but Frank had forbidden the teachers and pupils from helping me. Luckily, they helped me sometimes anyway. I was supposed to walk everywhere with the crutches, even on school outings, but luckily the teachers kept a wheelchair in secret.

From time to time, some of the teachers would take me to their homes for lunch and to spend the afternoon there. No one was waiting for me at home. Frank was working at that time and he did not know whether I was there or not. My friends helped me whenever they could. Once a week I went to my schoolfriend Tanja's house for lunch. She and her family were very nice to me. I felt very comfortable there. The three sisters were never beaten, insulted or kicked by their parents. The family was also very devout. They prayed before every meal and sometimes I went with them to church.

I did not talk to them about my problems with Frank for a long time, but one day I dared to tell Tanja's mother what life was like at home. I warned her that Frank must never know that I had told her. I quickly regretted telling her though because I had a strong feeling that she would tell him. I was right. Tanja's mother did speak to Frank and he, of course, denied everything as usual. And, as usual, he beat me for telling her and banned me from going there ever again. I did not want to go there anymore anyway because I was ashamed of having spoken to Tanja's mother. And I was sure that the family would not want to have anything to do with me now because Tanja's mother would think me a liar and a thief, which is what Frank had told her, even though she knew that I had never stolen anything from her or lied to her. It broke my heart. Every time I dared to ask for help, the people went straight to Frank! Did they really believe he would admit what he had done?

Hanging out with friends was no longer as much fun as it used to be. There was now only one friend with whom I could speak openly, because she was regularly raped by her father and we understood each other. We talked about our suffering, our dreams and our desires. We wrote poems and showed them to each other. We talked about our dream man and our future. We agreed on everything. We decided to concentrate on our schoolwork so we would get fantastic grades and go to high school, then study and work, live in a beautiful house and later start a family with our dream partners. We wanted to become independent so that we could look after ourselves because we were determined not to become dependent on someone else. We gave each other courage, stability and strength. Thinking about my younger siblings and Niara in Mali also gave me strength to keep going.

CHAPTER 15

trembling

The yellow dog: Did the beatings ever stop?

After my suicide attempt, I started yelling at Frank whenever he hit me. I asked him if he enjoyed beating up a helpless disabled child and asked what kind of a man he was. He looked at me horrified then and stopped. When he was drunk, he always felt sorry for beating me and apologized. He told me once that deep in his heart he loved me. He also told me about his father, who had beaten him when he was young, and once almost beat him to death. His father had forced him to steal. I realized that Frank was only doing what he had learned from his father, but it hurt my soul when he did it to me. I told him to talk to me gently and explain things to me. I told him that I was the child and he was the adult and that the way he treated me hurt me very much.

We would reconcile and he would go to bed, but the next day when he got up he would have forgotten the conversation we had had the night before and would start attacking me again. His attacks were unpredictable and could happen anywhere – he beat me in the pharmacy, in the supermarket, in the car, on the street. He even beat me in the sauna, where he took me every Sunday. I hated going to the sauna because you had to undress. I was ashamed to be naked, especially because of my skinny legs and deformed body, and I was also disgusted by the sight of other naked bodies! He would slap me, hit my head or punch me somewhere on my body. He wanted me to exercise 24 hours a day and, because I could not do it, I always got beaten. I did my exercises every evening before bed, but only if I was alone. I would move my legs back and forth and massage them, but of course he did not believe me, and he would call me a liar and hit me. He would beat me if the change from the shopping was wrong. I knew that I had given him the right change, but he often counted wrong or did not see that a coin had rolled away somewhere.

I was busy all day doing everything right. I cleaned everything several times, I checked everything over and over, and then I did not touch anything until he came home. I did not sit down and I did not eat anything. I would stand by the kitchen window, hoping for praise – surely he would be able to see that everything was clean, and that I was a hardworking child. But Frank would come in, look around, cut a slice of bread, eat it and then hit me because he had seen a crumb! He would claim I hadn't done the cleaning. When I told him I had just done it, he would hit me for answering back.

I cried every night when I was alone in my bed – not because of the physical pain, but for the insults, the humiliations, for the arbitrariness and hatred. Every day, every hour, every minute and every second, my heart was shattered again and again. I didn't cry in front of him. In his opinion, only cowards cried.

I received letters from my brother Madu, but those letters only hurt me more because he was not there to protect me. No one was there! When I wrote back, I always said I was fine because Frank read my letters too.

I had a problem with my hands. Sometimes they would shake. I never used to know why, but at some point, I realized that the shaking was related to Frank. I noticed that when I knew Frank was far away, my hands trembled less. And it seemed that my hands knew when he was coming back, because I worked out that the shaking began about an hour before he came home, and the closer he was, the more violent the trembling became. I wanted to learn how to handle this. So, when the trembling started in the evening, I would estimate the time of his arrival. Then I would stay quietly in the living room for a while and read a book or watch television. As soon as the trembling became stronger, I would clear up slowly so that he would not know I had been there. Then I would calmly brush my teeth and go to my room, take off my leg braces and pull on my pajamas. I would get into bed, count to three and then turn out the light. Frank only drove old cars, usually of the same make, and those cars made a distinctive sound. A few minutes after I turned out the light, I would hear his car in the distance. The sound would come closer, he would turn once to park in front of the house, pull the handbrake, get out, slam the door and walk to the house. I would hear him pull out his keys and unlock the door, hear how he closed the door behind him, opened the second door and called me. I did not answer! I pulled the blanket over my head. He would open my door and call me and I would pretend to be fast asleep. Then he would close the door and go away. My strategy worked! It meant that during the week, I was able to stay out of his way. But at the weekends he was always there, and if he went somewhere, I had to go with him. Sometimes I could read perplexity in his face and I rejoiced at it because he could not work out what was going on, and I suddenly felt superior to him.

CHAPTER 16

the last beating

The yellow dog: How did you escape?

One day, Frank had surgery on his knee and had to stay at home. I always used to get up at 5 am but he stormed into my room before my alarm went off and roared, "You ungrateful bastard!" Then he pulled the blanket off me and started hitting me like a crazy thing. He took the full laundry basket and threw it at me, then he took my crutch and hit my face with it, stepped on me and said, "You wanted to starve me. I do so much for you and you cannot even buy bread for me when I am sick!" When he left the room, I sat there looking at the clock. It was only 4 am! I was so angry that I had been beaten for nothing again. I packed my bag for school, took my savings, went to the bus stop and cried. I was determined that that would be the last time in this life that Frank or anyone else would beat me up. I planned to go to the railway station after school and take a train away from that place. Slowly, the bus station filled up. A friend looked at me and asked what had happened. I said nothing and got on the bus. When I arrived at school and my friend saw me, she knew immediately what had happened. It was hard to ignore my wounds and swollen face.

I told my friend about my plan to run away and she advised me to speak to a teacher instead. But which one? I was afraid they would not believe me and send me back to Frank. I burst into tears. A teacher saw me crying and came over to me. When she saw my face, it frightened her. She wanted to know who had done that to me. I told her it was Frank and that he was always beating me, but that this time he had been even more violent than before. The teacher went with me to the headmaster and I could see that his heart bled for me when he saw my face. I told him everything and he got angry at Frank and at the youth welfare office. At first, I was afraid that he too would call Frank and just send me back to him. That would have been the end of me because by now the whole school knew. But the headmaster said he used to be a policeman and was familiar with domestic violence and he promised me that he would not let anyone send me back to Frank. He picked up the phone and called the woman from the youth welfare office and told her what had happened. I have no idea what she said on the other end, but the headmaster got even angrier and told her that I was standing right in front of him and that he could see that I had been beaten up and he expected her to get me into a facility that same day, otherwise he would make her life difficult.

The woman went away to search for a place for me. The headmaster said that I could not attend classes in that state and asked if there was anyone I could trust. I gave him the phone number of Frank's sister, Sylvia. The headmaster called Sylvia and told her what had happened and asked her if she would be willing to look after me until the woman from the youth welfare office found a place for me. He assured her that I would have a place before the end of the day. She agreed, and a teacher took me to her house. When Sylvia saw me, she immediately took me in her arms and comforted me. She made me tea and called her husband, because she too was afraid. When her husband saw me, he almost started crying, because he had not realized how bad my situation was. Sylvia packed a bag with some clothes for me. She was scared the whole time that Frank might suddenly show up. We waited nervously for the phone call. Finally, it came. The woman from the youth welfare office had found a place for me.

Sylvia and her sister, who also brought clothes for me, drove me to the care home and helped me put my clothes in the closet. I did not understand what had just happened. It was all too much for me and I was exhausted. But I could also sense that I was not going to see Sylvia or her little sister ever again, although they both promised to keep in touch when they said goodbye and said they would be there for me. Before they left, they gave me money and hugged me.

I lay down and slept until the next day. The next morning, I felt as if I was in a trance. Everything around me was dark! I did not know where I was, who these people were or what had happened. I asked someone if I could make a phone call. A young woman took me to the telephone, and I called Sylvia. Sylvia was not pleased that I had called her. She told me that Frank had threatened her, saying that if she kept in touch with me, one of her own children might disappear one day. She wished me all the best but said I should not phone her anymore and then she hung up. I never heard from her again.

CHAPTER 17

Refuge

The yellow dog: So you were free. What was the new place like?

I went up to my new room and slept. I slept for a very, very long time. Eventually someone woke me up to tell me I had to eat! I went down to the kitchen, but I could not eat anything. A woman said to me, "You have to eat something, you haven't eaten anything since yesterday." I tried a little, but I just could not get it down. I started crying and said, "Please don't hit me" and covered my face with my arms. The woman said, "We don't do that. We don't hurt people here." She sat down and explained to me where I was and who she was. Then we went to the office and she told me I was safe and that Frank could not do anything to me anymore. But I did not believe her, because there were only women there. She told me she was in close contact with the police but I was still scared. I could not believe that everything was over so suddenly. Sure, I wanted to get away from Frank, but I did not want Sylvia to disappear from my life. Who would I go to if I wasn't well? Nobody knew me as well as she did! And was I not allowed to see my cousins again, just because I wanted to be free from the violence?

Over the next few days, I thought I saw Frank everywhere. It was never actually him, but still, I expected him to be there every second and I could not rest. This restlessness would not leave me.

Everyone told me not to worry. Some of the residents told me that they too had experienced exactly the same paranoia when they first arrived. After a few days, I dared to go to the front door, but never alone. I flinched whenever someone raised their voice, slammed a door or made a sudden hand movement. I lacked the courage to say anything because I was afraid of confrontation. I spent most of the time in my room.

Luckily, Emma, a girl I had known at school was there too. We had just started getting to know one another at school when she suddenly disappeared. Although Emma was a lot older than me, we got on very well. I admired her very much. She was very attractive and when she laughed, her whole being glowed. She was tall and slender and was always showing off her sexy body. Her beautiful dark-blond hair was always nicely groomed and her makeup perfect. Emma came into my room, gave me a hug and talked to me for a long time. She encouraged me and told me about the horrible experiences she had to go through with her family. Emma was born into a very strict religious family, so she was completely isolated from the modern world. The role of women was like in the Middle Ages. They had to wear their long hair in a braid, they could only wear knee-length skirts or dresses, and their role was to serve men. If they did not obey, they were violently punished and all this on the grounds that it was God's will.

After a while, when Frank did not turn up, I started to feel freer. I dared to go out of the house and began to take in my surroundings more clearly. The house stood on a huge plot of land. There were many different buildings, including the main house, where the nuns who ran the place lived, and a large kitchen, in which the young people could also be trained. Next to it was a house for boys. There was also a special school there. There were two nuns in charge of the house I was living in. I met the girls from my group and listened to their stories. I found their experiences crueler than mine. Listening to their stories, I realized that I was not a bad person. I even wondered whether cruelty was part of everyday life in Germany – otherwise surely there would be no need for a facility like the one I was in. The reason I had never gone to the police about Frank was because his best friend was a cop who lived next door to us. This policeman also regularly beat his wife and children. Once, I spoke to his wife briefly and another neighbor, who got along with the policeman, called him and he soon came over and beat her up! I could hear her screaming. Frank told me over and over that if I ever called the police, the first thing they would do would be to call Frank! I asked myself many times why he had taken me in at all. He would have had a much easier life if he had just left me in Volta or sent me back to my family.

The support workers at the center taught me about human rights. I realized that I had been wrong all those years. Frank had no right to beat me up and bully me every day. One day, the center invited Frank to a meeting. He came with his mother to prove his innocence. I knew that she would deny everything I said because she was always on his side, even though she knew how he had treated me. Frank was everything to her and he often told me that his dream girl had to be just like his mother. My support workers knew that Frank and his mother would try to portray me as a liar, but I also knew that the head of the youth center was on my side and would protect me. My support worker prepared me for the meeting and I trusted her. Frank and his mother kept accusing me and we did not come to any kind of resolution.

My heart broke when I felt that Frank was relieved not to have me in his house anymore and that staying with him was no longer a possibility. Of course, I was glad that the beatings had stopped and that no one was yelling at me and insulting me but, at the same time, I found it hard to let go. Frank was my German family. He came only once more: Just before Christmas, he left a basket of fruit at the door and went away again. Knowing that from then on I had no family hurt me so much. This thought would not leave me.

Up until the summer vacation, I carried on taking the bus to my old school, even though my support workers were encouraging me to change schools. It was a very long journey – two hours there and back – but I did not want to lose my friends. We wanted to graduate together. But I was a very different person now. I was so empty inside and without joy. My friends noticed it too. Eventually, I realized that I could not cope with the long school journey and switched to a school not far from the center. Walking was now an even greater torment. I used to break out in a sweat after every step and had to take regular breaks. Everything I did seemed to take forever. Although the school was only ten to fifteen minutes away, it sometimes took me an hour and a half to get there. Even when I left the house earlier, I always arrived late.

At the care home, I was supposed to do everything the others did. I had to clean a room once a week, and shop and cook for my group once a week (eight people, including the staff). But I needed much, much longer to do everything! The staff noticed this, of course. I made a big effort because I was desperate to stay there. I had only just got there and, in any case, I had always done everything on my own. However, there was usually someone who took pity on me and helped me, and sometimes they would arrange for the transport service to take me to school. I found some nice teachers who would take me to school sometimes. My roommates and the staff at the center also helped me, but they made it clear that this could not become a permanent state of affairs. I would only be able to stay at the care home if I could live independently. One of the support workers also told me that I would only be allowed to stay there until I left school, because it was a home for children and teenagers with learning difficulties and not a home for people with disabilities. The staff never had any trouble with me. On the contrary, they trusted me because I was reliable. I never misbehaved, either in Africa or in Germany. I never got into trouble, I never went out alone in the evening and I didn't drink alcohol (except the time I tried to kill myself). And I was always polite to everyone. I spoke softly and I was often asked to speak up. I always followed rules and stuck to agreements. I went to bed alone and always got up on time, my room was always tidy, I was always punctual and careful. When there were conflicts, I always strived for harmony, because I hated to see anyone crying or suffering, and above all I was always honest with everyone, sometimes too honest. To this day, Frank is the only person who has ever thought I was a horrible person. As time went on, I wondered more and more why he adopted me. But I never found an answer.

CHAPTER 18

Training

The yellow dog: So what happened when you left school?

After spending a year in the care home, I finished school. I was sad about graduating because I knew I would have to leave the center. I was registered to do a three-year training program at a boarding school for disabled children and adolescents. I did not want to go there, but there was no other place for me.

When it was time to leave the care home, I said goodbye to my roommates, and then Sandra, my favorite support worker, drove me to my new home. She brought my luggage to my room hugged me and left. I wanted to keep in touch with her afterwards, but she broke off contact with me because she was no longer responsible for me.

I cried at first, but when I calmed down, I unpacked and made my single room as cozy as I could. After that I went to see my new support workers, who were very nice to me. Later that day, I saw that a sweet boy lived in the room next to mine, but I did not dare to say hello to him. When he noticed me, he came to me and invited me to his room. His name was David and his roommate was called Christian. We got on well and talked for a long time about all kinds of things and watched a movie. After the movie I was very tired and went to bed. The next day I met the gang of five girls, and I immediately took to Jill. Jill and I did everything together and she showed me round the center. I also found Julia, a red-haired girl I had met when I visited the place before.

Over the following days I had to complete paperwork and I explored the boarding school. I was amazed at how big it was. Everything was under one roof: kindergarten, various types of school, training facilities, a hospital, residential groups divided by age and education level, many different leisure and sports activities, even an indoor swimming pool and a climbing wall. If you wanted, you could go out for shopping, but otherwise every group could have a choice of meals three times a day from the canteen.

At some point, a member of staff told me I would not be able to start my training program straight away, because there was no space for me. I would have to spend a year doing a pre-vocational traineeship first. I was very upset about this, because that was not the deal! Unfortunately, there was nothing I could do about it. I did not want to do the pre-vocational training because it was so basic. For the first time in my life, I went to my classes reluctantly. The only good thing was that the class was very small – just six students. This was part of the concept on which the facility was built: Fewer students meant focused attention for each individual. But after a few weeks, I got very annoyed. The lessons were boring, and I had nothing in common with my classmates. I was being forced to learn to read and write all over again and to learn one plus one. The others in the class could not do it because of their disabilities and most of them were taking the class for the second time and still did not understand the lessons. I did not say anything at the beginning because I did not want to offend anyone.

However, after a few months I could no longer stay quiet and started to rebel for the first time in my life. I refused to spend a year learning to read and write again. I began to challenge the teacher. I was only engaged with the few subjects that I found interesting. In all the other subjects, I started to leave the class when I felt like it, or I tried to go to sleep. One day I deliberately put my feet on the table and the teacher exploded and called my support workers to complain about my behavior. He did not know that I had already spoken to them about the lessons. The teacher and a support worker held a meeting. My support worker came to class and we sat down to talk.

At the end of the conversation, we agreed that the teacher should support my progress because I did not have any mental limitations. It meant I could help the teacher with the class, so the second half of the year became more interesting.

The lesson plan also included several hours of therapy. I chose physio, conversation and occupational therapy. Occupational therapy was not necessary, but I liked my therapist and it meant I was able to spend time with her. My physiotherapist, Lena, was horrified when I told her that I had never really had physiotherapy before. Lena and the support workers got a wheelchair for me, as everyone could see that walking was pure torment and made no sense anymore. I got a new lease of life when I sat in the wheelchair. All at once, I could move fast and take in my surroundings on the move. It gave me a sense of freedom. For a while I tried to alternate between using the leg braces and the wheelchair, but at some point, I decided to use the wheelchair all the time – because it did not hurt, it did not make me sweat and, above all, I could at last move faster than a tortoise. Lena also took me to see an orthopedic surgeon because she was worried about my right shoulder, my right knee and left hip. The orthopedist had no idea what was wrong with me and suggested stiffening all my joints. Lena did not see any sense in this because the operations would make my life even more complicated. Since I trusted her, I declined the orthopedist's offer.

CHAPTER 19

Mornings

The yellow dog: Did you enjoy life at the boarding school?

I settled into life at the center very quickly. I had some support workers I trusted and who gave me very good life advice. They became my new family. I could go and talk to them about anything. But I never talked about what I experienced with Frank or about my family in Africa. For a while, I also kept in touch with my old friends, but eventually I lost contact with them.

The mornings were a problem for me though. Every morning my whole body hurt. I felt as if I was in a trance. I was awake and not awake at the same time. My thoughts were somewhere else and my head felt like a prison, full of circling thoughts that I could not grasp. Why did I feel as if I had been beaten, when nobody was hitting me? And why did my head hurt so much that I could not think. I often had stomach problems. The hole in my heart was getting bigger and darker. I never said anything. I went into the day as if nothing had happened. If I had a headache in the morning, I just ignored it until it got worse. Then I would go to my room and made everything dark, because the brightness made it worse. I tried to fall asleep somehow, but the pain would get worse and worse. The headaches felt as if someone was opening my skull while I was fully conscious and pulling my brain out bit by bit with tweezers, or as if someone was boring into my skull with a pneumatic drill.

The day after one of these seizures, I always felt light and very well and would take the day in a very calm, relaxed manner. With Frank, I sometimes suffered such intense pain that I fainted and woke up in the hospital. The only thing I could remember in the hospital was that I had had a terrible headache and that I had suddenly seen a lot of white stars just before I lost consciousness. The doctors said I was suffering from migraines, but I always forgot to mention the heavy blows Frank gave me. The doctors tried everything, but nothing helped. I still wonder why I never mentioned that I was constantly being hit on the head. Maybe that would have been my chance to get away from Frank much sooner.

At the boarding school, the others always thought that I was in a bad mood because I had such a serious expression. Sometimes I looked so grim that they all fled from me! But I was not in a bad mood. I felt as if I'd been beaten up. I felt the way I had when Frank used to beat me – the same pain in the same places! I could never explain that, because he was no longer there and no one hit me in there. I was just never mentally present in the mornings. I was trapped somewhere else. After a few hours, I would come back to myself and the pain would disappear.

At some point, a doctor who is working there realized that I had lactose and sorbitol intolerance, which explained why I always had such severe stomach problems. When I started making changes to my diet, the stomach pains got better. Another problem I had was that I would often become extremely tired all of a sudden and be forced to take a nap. Later, the doctor told me I had almost no red blood cells in my blood and that usually I would not have any color in my face either, but with my dark skin it was very difficult to see that. I was given tablets. Unfortunately, they did not work, but at least I now knew why I was so tired. In any case, I never slept well at night. I was always tense and aware of every sound.

After school, I would do my homework and then play sports or do pottery. My support workers encouraged me to do a higher qualification, so I took the entry examination for the business school and passed straight away.

CHAPTER 20

Heroes

The yellow dog: Was there anyone at the boarding school who inspired you?

I saw so many diseases and disabilities at that center. Some of the conditions were cruel, but the people coped very well. They had beautiful charismas, as if they were guarding a secret. My room neighbor David, for example, was someone I admired very much. David had had a swimming accident. When I met him, he was walking, but before that he had been in a wheelchair and the doctors had told him that he would never walk again. He was so determined that he trained hard every day on his own and then suddenly one day he could walk.

Jill and I became best friends. She had dark brown hair and brown eyes. She always wore glasses and loose dresses. We were the same age. She came from Croatia originally and her parents had fled with her to Germany because of the Bosnian War. Jill took to me immediately too. At some point, without going into details, I told her that my real family in Africa had given me away and that my adoptive father was violent to me. She said to me, "OK, I am your mama now." She told me that she had had a cerebral hemorrhage a few years ago and had fallen into a coma. After that she had to learn everything again: how to speak, eat and drink by herself and even how to walk. According to the doctors, her chances of recovery were very slim. But because of her strong will and faith, she had fought her way back to life! When I met her, she was already walking, but she still had slight balance and motor issues and she spoke slowly. I admired her very much for her willpower.

I got to know Slato, a young wheelchair user, and I quickly made him my role model, because he did everything for himself, despite the wheelchair. He went shopping, cleaned his room, did his exercises, did his training courses and already knew what he was going to do afterwards. I also had a good chat with him. For some reason, many people did not like him, but he did not care and went his own way. He was in a wheelchair because one day, after taking drugs, he had jumped from a tower block thinking he could fly like a bird! I wanted to go through my life like Slato. I saw everything he did and did it too. Like him, I went shopping, and did sports like climbing, swimming, archery and fitness training – although I soon gave up the fitness training because it did not go well! Later, I did handcycling with a few other wheelchair users. I started to cook because I did not like the canteen food. I tried to structure my life. I would spend my free evenings with my friends and at 10 pm I would go to my room. Usually, I would read for a bit and think about my life before going to bed.

The business school gave me confidence. I enjoyed learning. I got on very well with the staff and my roommates. Almost everyone liked me because I was always cheerful and friendly. At this time, I had changed my look and wore very colorful clothes. I liked almost everyone there too, and the school became my home for a while. Through the school I could also travel once a year, for example to Turkey or St. Moritz. During the summer vacation I also did a lot with the staff. And I saw the conversation therapist once a week. His name was Mr. Adler. He was small with grey hair and very handsome. We got on well right away. I was always happy when it was time to see him. He became like the father I never had. He always encouraged me when I was unwell. However, I could not speak in detail about my bad experiences, because I was not yet ready, and he did not force me. Mr. Adler made the best espresso in the world! After drinking one cup I was fully awake and could hear my heart beating.

I enjoyed the first three years at the boarding school and had a lot of fun. But from the third year, I started feeling as if I was somehow trapped. I felt as if my life was repeating itself, it was so calm and normal. I now missed the trips with Frank. They were much more exciting because they were not planned.

I could only be with my gang of girls on weekdays, but at the weekends and during the vacations all my friends went home to their families. On these days, I felt alone even if I kept myself busy. Occasionally, a friend would take me home with them for a weekend, or for Christmas, so I wouldn't have to spend it alone at the center. I spent one Christmas at Mr. Adler's house and met his children and girlfriend. Julia took me home with her for a weekend too. She was a single mother, and I got on very well with her little daughter. Julia became one of the most important people in my life. She taught me not to take life too seriously and I admired her very much.

Another time I spent Christmas with a lad who was paralyzed as a result of a swimming accident. There I also met Chloé. Chloé was the first person I had met in ages who spoke French. We went for a walk and she showed me around her city. Chloé grew up in France. She told me that although France and Germany are not far away from each other, they have very different cultures. I already knew a bit about French culture from Ivette. Chloé's life has not been easy either. Arriving in a strange country in her teens, she faced some racist reactions because she does not look German and she did not speak German very well at the time. She is like a beautiful Egyptian princess, with brown eyes and dark hair. She told me that many people insulted her and said: "Go back to your country" even though she is German too and has a German father.

Chloé and I have kept in touch, even though she lives 500 miles away from my town. At first, we wrote letters to each other, but now that everyone has cell phones, we often talk on the phone. I have been to her house several times by train and she has also visited me. I trust her. We have similar characters and have had some similar experiences. For instance, she told me she once went to a friend's house and this friend asked her to wait in her room while she had dinner with her family. Chloé was very confused and I understood her completely because I had had the same experience and found it confusing too! In Mali, you always share your food when someone comes to visit.

Chloé's German friends banned us from speaking French because they did not understand it. So the only time we could speak French together was when we were alone or with her family.

I saw lots of disabled people at the center and I soon realized that the vast majority had ended up like that because of illness or accident. But they were fighting for life and did not give up. All those people were heroes to me. No one is safe. There will always be accidents and illnesses. At the end of the day, it is about what you make of them. The worst thing about their situation was that most of them had lost their friends from before. I do not understand why that should be so. People's personalities have nothing to do with their disability.

Photo by Pascal Mathieu

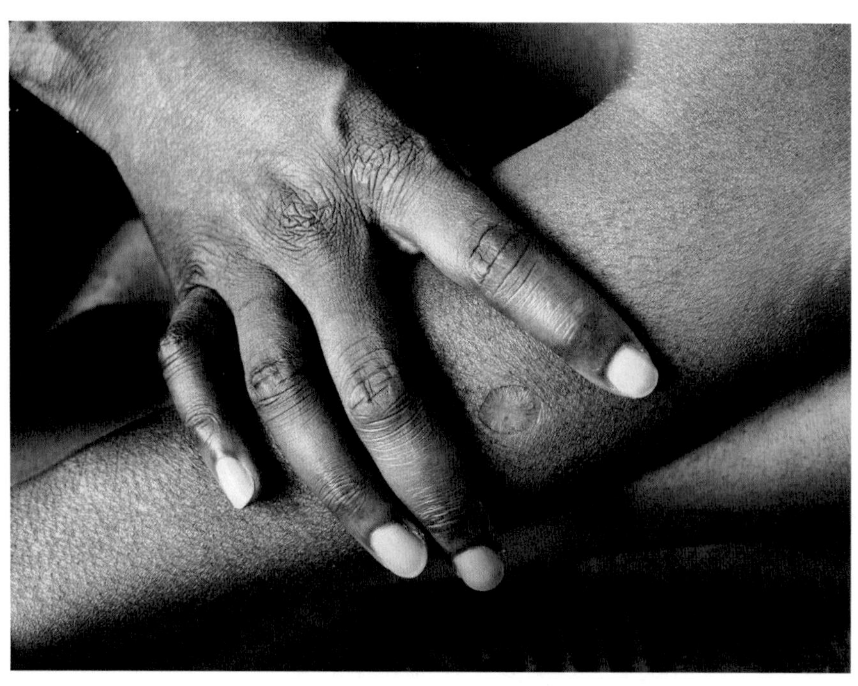

Photo by Pascal Mathieu

CHAPTER 21

Coming of age

The yellow dog: What happened when you turned eighteen?

When I became an adult, I had to start dealing with the authorities myself. I also realized that I had to take responsibility for myself – if I got into trouble, then I would be held accountable. So it was very important for me to abide by the rules and not draw attention to myself for the wrong reasons. After a while, my life was filled with rules: the rules of the places I lived in and the rules I imposed on myself.

When I turned 18, I had to apply for funding to cover the cost of my stay at the center and for money to travel with my class or for new clothes. These were things that my support workers used to do for me. As my support workers trusted me and could see that I was able to manage independently, they offered me the choice of moving to an apartment outside the center. I was delighted because I was tired of being surrounded by disease all the time.

All the bad diseases I came across at the center made me realize that my disability was nothing by comparison. At the end of the day, I was doing very well. And I never had reason to complain about my disability because it was a part of me and I didn't think it should ever hold me back from doing something I wanted to do. One day, I met a young man in an electric wheelchair. He had muscular dystrophy and the doctors had told him he could die at any moment. Despite this, he was calmly getting an education and planning his future. I had a lot of respect for him. He gave me so much hope. But in the long term I couldn't bear to be surrounded by sick people anymore, because it depressed me.

Once I moved into my apartment, I would go into town on weekends. I met interesting people, most of them students, and a few of them came from Africa. It was the first time since coming to Germany that I had had friends from Africa. I felt so comfortable with them. We listened to the same music and shared the same worldview. Like me, most of them were committed to fighting the injustices of this world. We went to reggae festivals together and rocked the night away, although I never drank alcohol because I didn't like the taste and even the smell of it was enough to make me tipsy! Of course, everyone noticed that I was different, but my disability was never an issue for these new friends. They liked me as a person. Even with them, though, I did not really talk about my experiences.

CHAPTER 22

Falling in love

The yellow dog: What about romantic relationships?

I was once very much in love with a young man with blond hair and light blue eyes. I always called him Sonny Boy. He was doing his civilian service in the center and looked after the children there. For me, it was love at first sight! Whenever we met in the hallway, my heart would skip a beat and I would grin at him. He always smiled too, but he wasn‘t sure yet. Sonny Boy was quite surprised when he realized that he felt more for me.

We agreed to give ourselves time and to get to know each other slowly. I thought his fears and worries were justified because he had never had a girlfriend in a wheelchair before. He lived nearby and used to pick me up on weekends. After several dates he was ready for the next step and he admitted his strong feelings for me over a romantic dinner. I could not believe my luck, as I had been sure he would decide against me. Shortly afterwards, he introduced me to his friends and family. I immediately got on well with his friends and his mother. Only his father behaved strangely. He reminded me a little of Frank‘s father.

Sonny Boy was very empathetic and affectionate. I had never known such sensual intimacy before, but I started to vomit after we made love. I always thought I had eaten something bad or had an infection. Sonny Boy found it strange too, but he never said anything about it. Our relationship took place in secret because he worked in center. Not even my best friend Jill knew about it. My girlfriends only found out by chance one day when they came to visit me in hospital. I had been admitted with suspected appendicitis and had to have an operation. They were with me there when Sonny Boy suddenly came in with a huge bouquet of flowers.

When I came out of hospital, he took me home and looked after me. These days that I spent with Sonny Boy were wonderful, but did not last long. One day, he told me that he had to go abroad for three months. The trip had been planned before we met, and we agreed to endure the separation together. Sonny Boy was my first relationship and first love. He noticed that something was the matter with me, but because I never told him about the hell I had left behind me, he didn't know what it was. I did try to tell him once or twice, but the words stuck like a lump in my throat.

When Sonny Boy was abroad, I yearned for him and wrote him love poems. I was sure he would be happy to receive them, but the opposite was true – he ended our relationship by email because my emotional love letters were too much for him. I could not understand his behavior and was heartbroken.

The second time I fell in love was at a reggae festival. My friend Katharina and I were walking through the grounds after putting our bags in the tent, when I saw a very handsome young man in the crowd and fell in love with him instantly. He had such beautiful blue eyes and short, dark-blond hair. When he saw me, he handed me a bottle. I thought it was orange juice, but when I drank from it, I could taste alcohol and I made a face and gave it back to him. He introduced himself as Oliver and asked my name. I just had time to say "Hawa" before I lost him in the crowd. It all happened so fast. My mind was full of him and I really wanted to see him again, but how could I find him when there were nearly 30,000 people there? An inner voice told me that if we belonged together, then we would find each other again.

Later, Katharina and I found a nice place in a meadow and sat down. We were chatting, when someone suddenly grabbed me from behind. Oliver! He and his friend had been looking for me. He asked me what I wanted to drink and when he came back with my orange juice, the other two tactfully left us alone. We went to the concert area and took a seat in the space for wheelchair users. We talked and talked, about God and the world. We only had eyes for each other. Everything around us became quiet. I felt very powerful, beautiful emotions, destiny and a deep sense of connection. I did not know what those strong feelings and thoughts meant, but I immediately knew that he had a good heart and I felt he was serious about me. I could tell from the way he looked at me that he had fallen hopelessly in love with me. All these years I had dreamed of this moment, and now my wish was fulfilled. I could not take my eyes off his face and his beautiful blue eyes. The evening was magical and passed quickly, even though we talked until dawn. When he brought me to my tent, we exchanged phone numbers. The next morning when I woke up, I thought I had imagined the whole thing, but then I got a text message from him.

I thought about Oliver all the way home. He lived about 400 miles north of me, but he planned to come and see me the following weekend. In the meantime, he called me every day. He was very sweet – he complimented me, said he missed me and that he was looking forward to spending the weekend with me. I even spoke to his mother one time, who seemed very nice. This was all very new to me. I had had boyfriends before, but they had been reticent about their feelings towards me. Now I was so excited about the weekend that I did not know what to cook or what to wear. At one point I even started to have doubts about the whole thing, and did not trust my feelings anymore, but a friend calmed me down.

The closer the weekend came, the more nervous I got. I also wondered what such a handsome man wanted from me. Why wasn't he put off by my wheelchair? Then he arrived, and he was so sweet! He gave me flowers and a nice dress, which was unfortunately a little too big, but it was the thought that mattered. We talked and talked, and found we shared the same opinion on very many things. I told Oliver that honesty was very important to me, because that was the only way I could understand him and help him too. I did not want any jealous scenes because that was not something I was used to, and I did not want to have a traditional relationship, but rather an equal one. I wanted to be his best friend, not just his girlfriend. He liked this idea and agreed with me.

I told Oliver a bit of my story because I wanted him to know why I was the way I was. I quickly realized how good it was for me to talk about my experience, but Oliver became quiet and started crying. He said I should stop because he could not bear to hear what I was saying. He said the things that had happened to me hurt his soul. He hated Frank and said he never wanted to see him because otherwise he would freak out. And he said that from now on I would be safe – he would never let anyone hurt me again. I could tell straight away that he was serious, and I was so glad to have a protector. He told me I was the most beautiful, strong and honest woman he had ever met and that he would be my family from now on. No one had ever said anything like this to me before. I could not believe it and, at first, I thought he was just saying it to distract me.

Oliver told me that when he was a little boy, his father had shot himself and his funeral had taken place on his birthday, so every year he is reminded of this horrible event. Every time Oliver told me about his dad, I could see the little Oliver. His eyes shone and I could see he missed him so much!

That first weekend with Oliver was so wonderful that parting was painful. Afterwards, we phoned each other every day, and on weekends I went to visit him. I met his friends and family and was welcomed everywhere. I got to know his little sister and we hit it off immediately. I also got on well with his mother because we already knew each other from speaking on the phone. His grandma and grandpa liked me and even Oliver's stepfather said I was nice. Oliver was surprised about that. His friends were fond of me too. Of course, I was glad that everyone was so friendly, but I could not understand their enthusiasm towards me.

CHAPTER 23

Kindness

The yellow dog: Were there no arguments?

The first time I heard Oliver yell at his mother, I was so shocked, because I had never seen a child shout at his mother before. I told him to stop and he looked at me in a scary way, got angry and stormed out of the kitchen. I did not know what to make of this behavior, but his mother said he just needed to calm down and then he would come right back. So we carried on talking as if nothing had happened. When Oliver came back in, he apologized to his mother and they both kissed and said they were fond of each other. Later, we talked about it and I told him that I had never experienced anything like that before. In Africa, if a child dares to talk to his mother or father like that, the punishment will be severe! To disagree with one's parents is taboo. And I hate to think what Frank would have done to me in that situation. Oliver understood me, but he said he and his family love each other and that having arguments and making up was normal for them. He said I should see them as a temperamental Italian family. I considered this and decided that as long as they were able to make peace again afterwards, it was fine for me too.

Oliver's grandmother was very cute. The first time she met me, she pursued me all day with a banana. Even when I left, she still wanted me to take the banana with me. She thought Africans loved bananas and she just wanted to make me happy. She was so naive, it made us laugh.

I will never forget how kind Oliver's grandfather was. He was a good man. He hid Jews from Poland during World War II and saved their lives. When he worked in his garden, a one-legged robin would sit on his head. Once, I went out to the garden and the wheel on my wheelchair got stuck in the sand. He said, "Wait, honey, I'm coming," and he got me out of there as if I was in a wheelbarrow! Unfortunately, he ended up with Alzheimer's. One day, on his birthday, we went to a restaurant. At some point he turned to me and smiled as if it was the first time he'd met me. He held out his hand and introduced himself, saying, "Hello, my name is Willy-Bocou. Pleased to meet you." He thought I was an African queen who had come especially for his birthday. "I am delighted that you came all this way to visit me," he said and wished me a "good flight home to my kingdom."

I found it very hard to accept such sincere affection. I thought their kindness would lessen over time. One day, Oliver called me and said his mother and sister had bought plane tickets for us. They wanted to fly to Tunisia during the summer vacations and take me with them. I couldn't believe my luck! I asked him why they were doing this, because they did not know me that well. Oliver just said, "Because they like you and they want to spend the vacation with us." I was very happy and of course I was keen to travel again, and to see the sun and the sea.

When we arrived in Tunisia, a bus took us and the other tourists to the hotel. It was an all-inclusive trip – something very new to me. I had never had a vacation where I did not have to do anything except relax. I did try to relax, but my morning pain was worse, and I could not hide it. I was partly there and partly somewhere else. Something surrounded me and kept me trapped. I started wondering why I deserved to come on the trip. Why were they so kind to me? What did they want from me? I questioned everything and everyone during these phases. Oliver's family could see that something was wrong with me and thought I was in a bad mood. I was not in a bad mood but I could not explain it. I told Oliver that I felt as if I'd been beaten up and that everything hurt. Even he did not know what to make of that. Luckily, this phase did not last long, and the vacation was still very nice because we understood one another very well. Our bond became even stronger there.

Back in Germany, I fell again into a deep hole because I still did not know what to do or where to go. My love lived a long way away from me and I was trapped in the center about to start an apprenticeship that I didn't want to do. I started questioning everything again, even Oliver's feelings for me. I Asked myself what "love" was. How could he and his family love me at all? I assumed that he would break up with me soon and I did not want to experience the pain of rejection again, because my heart could not endure it. I could still feel the experience with Sonny Boy deep in my bones. But Oliver did not leave me. By now, we had been together for six months. He made me laugh and we continued to speak about everything. He explained many things that I did not know. He continued to take me everywhere and even carried me upstairs, no matter how many flights there were. We spent Christmas together and we still got on really well. I realized that his feelings for me were real. I tried to see each day positively, although I found it hard to see that my life was actually beautiful, full of love and harmony. Because it was so strange and new to me, I found it hard to accept.

Of course, Oliver and I also argued a lot. When he shouted at me, I became very frightened. I expected him to beat me up at any moment and my breathing would falter. But he never hit me. For me it was clear that if he did, I would leave him, but it was not in his nature – it was only my fear. Oliver would have loved it if I lived close to him, but I could not imagine living with him because I did not want to become dependent on him or to become a burden.

I spent my vacations and weekends at Oliver's house. I loved going there. I had never experienced such beautiful days in my life with so much love and security. I always helped his mother prepare meals and we went together to the market. She was a very good cook and her meals were always delicious. She often hugged me. Oliver used to give me massages. He had a very good feeling for tension and was able to dissolve blockages all over my neck, back and shoulders. But I tensed up again quickly afterwards. He always said I should just relax, but I could not. I had never been relaxed in my life. He still called me darling or tiger. Sadly, with him too, I always vomited when we became intimate, but he was very understanding. In fact, I started to vomit after almost every lovely family occasion –birthdays, Christmas, barbeques or just a dinner for two. I always felt a kind of stimulus overload. Everything around me started turning and I felt as if I was in a dream.

After more than a year, Oliver still had not ended our relationship and that made me angry inside! I couldn't believe that he was still with me after such a long time. One day, even though I knew he was preparing for his exams, I called him to end it because I could not believe that he still loved me. But he just laughed and told me that I wouldn't get rid of him that easily. Instead, he said I was sweet and that no matter what happened between us, he would never leave me. He said I could go through all kinds of theories in my head and throw all of them at him and he would still always love me. This time I really believed him. When I hung up, I realized that he was serious about me and, from then on, I trusted him completely.

But what about me? Did I love him? How could I know what love was? Had I ever been truly loved? I looked back over my life to see where I had been loved and by whom and I immediately thought of Niara, Kouami and all my younger siblings, and of Ivette and Sylvia. I remembered all my friends I laughed with and the wonderful times we spent together. I started to notice that everywhere I had been, people had shown me love. Sometimes love expresses itself in the form of a smile, or just a nice conversation or a friendly gesture. I saw that I was loved by a great many people. I thought of all the beautiful things Oliver said to me and I asked myself what if God had sent me all these people so that I could finally learn how to love, or to show me that I am a lovely person? I decided to take my relationship more seriously. I realized that love will withstand everything, and it is normal to argue – it doesn't mean that a relationship will become violent.

I remember the first time I screamed. I terrified myself because I did not even know that I was capable of screaming. Oliver looked at me in fright and asked me how it felt. We laughed about it. I was so glad that I could scream, because I always felt much easier afterwards, as if all the anger and rage that had accumulated over the years had been let out. We always argued when one of us was stressed.

Sometimes Oliver was stressed because he missed his dad and did not know what to do with the pain. I realized that that was all part of life and that it is healthy to express negative feelings.

At some point, though, my emotional and physical health worsened again. I was deeply unhappy, despite being loved. Everyone close to me noticed that I was getting worse and they all tried to find out what was wrong with me. I even went to see Oliver's stepfather, who was psychologist, but he could not help me because we were just talking about how to manage my life. I felt that his kind of therapy was not for me. I needed something else, but I did not know what.

I did not know why I should force myself to go out every morning. I felt an intense physical and mental pain. I could not concentrate on school or work, but I went every day anyway. I just wanted to die because my life felt so empty and hard. Oliver used to phone me every day and tried to encourage me. He did give me strength, but it never lasted long. I became even more sick and started looking for help because I thought there must be another way.

CHAPTER 24

Searching

The yellow dog: Did you find any answers?

I looked in books. I was trying to find out what was wrong with me, but I could not find my diagnosis. I only found all the conditions I did not have, and that included depression. I asked my doctor and he just said "psychosomatic!" In other words, everything was in my head. But then why did it affect my body? Can the spirit be that strong?

I had spent all the years after escaping from Frank trying to find my place in society and had repressed the bad experiences to be "normal." But I hope I have always been mentally alert. I have always been able to perceive my environment very clearly. I thought that was how it was for everyone. I started to ask "why" questions until I realized that life should be about more than just working and getting through each day.

By now I was back in the center about to start an apprenticeship as an industrial clerk – a nightmare for me – because I couldn't find anything else to do. Even though I had studied hard and done well in my exams, I had not been able to find a job. I had applied to very many companies, but all I got were rejections. I could not understand it. It could not have been because of my grades, because they were good. But I did not even get invited for interview and most of the companies didn't bother to reply at all. I thought it might have been because I was in a wheelchair, but several people told me it was probably also because of my skin color. I did not want to admit that my skin color might be a problem because that would mean that I would never have the chance to live a successful and independent life. I was painfully aware of my situation – disabled and with no family to support me – and now my skin color was to be an issue too?

What was I supposed to do? I did not want to do an apprenticeship at the center. All my friends had left and I didn't get on with the new support staff and students. The people there were so strange! I felt as if the wind had changed. I no longer felt alive and my mood was dark because I did not fit in and I could not escape. Why should I have to do an apprenticeship I did not want to do just because I had a disability and the society I lived in was not tolerant enough? I was fully integrated in Germany and I could speak and write the language very well, so I thought I would be able to find something on the normal job market that I would enjoy. Deep in my heart, I wanted to study but I did not know how to finance my studies because there was no one to support me, and the support I was entitled to did not cover all costs. I also wanted to do something creative or to help people in Africa, or work with children. I did not want to stay at the center. I had been there longer than anywhere else I had ever stayed. The time had come for me to move on.

One day a good friend told me about a nursing service, and he made an appointment for me. The people there listened to me and understood my problem. They told me that they would soon get me out of the center. And they did. A few days later, they called me to say they had found a job for me. I could not believe my luck! Hope started spreading inside me at last.

When I told the people in the employment office my good news, they congratulated me, but then told me I had to vacate my room within three days! I asked for an extension because I did not yet have an apartment of my own, but they said that was not their problem. I had been thrown out! I did not let it bother me for long though. I called some friends and one of them put me up for three months until I got my own apartment.

My job was in an office, but I didn't mind. I still wanted to study somehow, so I signed up for evening classes. At last my dream of a normal, independent life had come true!

However, after working in the office for a few years, it stopped being fun. My colleagues started bullying me. No matter what I did or didn't do, they always found a reason to turn against me and to bitch about me. Even when I moved to another office, my colleagues there started bitching about me too. It was always the women who started being mean towards me. I took everything personally and my self-esteem plummeted. Oliver was also affected by the situation because there was nothing he could do about my colleagues. My boss was overwhelmed by the difficult situation and had to sign me off work for a while. Soon afterwards, the company ran into problems and he was forced to dismiss a few people. I was one of them. Luckily, I still had my evening classes, so I focused on them. But inside me there was a strong sense of rejection and powerlessness that came from strangers telling me that I did not belong here. I really believed I did not belong here. Who was I and where did I belong?

I started reading a lot of books because I was convinced that someone must have found the meaning of life. I discovered so many different opinions. I could agree with some of them, but not others. It was a question that seemed to concern the whole of humanity. I began to develop my own theory about the meaning of life. Is life not individual? Can it be a blessing for me? Are we really like pack animals that need a guide at the top? Has the world ever been free? How did our early ancestors survive? Do we come from Africa or from the apes? Maybe we are descended from Adam and Eve, which would mean incest somehow, wouldn't it? Ultimately, are God and Satan just playing chess with mankind? I had plenty of friends to discuss these things with. I gathered information from lots of different sources and evaluated it against my own experiences and views.

In the end, the only thing I knew was that life was not a coincidence. Therefore, it was always important to have your own experience and to build your own opinion. No matter which decision you make, you have to make it in your own way and always be prepared to bear the responsibility for and consequences of your own actions.

CHAPTER 25

Disillusionment

The yellow dog: Did you ever go back to Mali without Frank?

I had many kind friends around me, and they made it possible for me to travel to Mali. Now that Frank was no longer in my life, I thought I could finally try to have a better relationship with my birth family and forget what had come between us. My love for them drew me back. The thought of seeing my family in Africa again always made me so happy that my condition improved at once. I had started to wonder whether my problems stemmed from the fact that I missed my family and I was homesick after not seeing them for almost seven years.

There was a problem now, though: The only address I had for my family was an old mailbox number, and the last letters I had sent had come back with the inscription "recipient unknown."

Oliver and a friend of mine called Uwe agreed to come with me to see if we could find them. We applied for visas, booked flights and arranged for vaccinations. I was very happy that I would finally get to see my family again. It would be the first time I had gone to Mali without Frank. And this time I was responsible for Oliver and Uwe and I had to make sure they got there and back safely.

I organized and planned our route. I have no idea where this basic trust in life came from, but I was sure everything would go well. I knew that nothing bad would happen to us in Mali, because everyone from Bamako to Niger knew my father. He was my entry key and security card. I decided we would go to Ségou first. A former German acquaintance of Frank's owned a travel company and hotel there and was also known everywhere in Mali. Ségou is a city to the northeast of Bamako. It attracts lots of visitors each year for the Festival on the River.

From Ségou we would somehow make our way to Gaya, either by car or by bus. I also remembered that my aunt Niara used to tell me, "Child, always take candies for the children on your travels, as they will bless your journey." At the airport in Germany, our tickets were simply exchanged for first class seats. A stroke of luck.

After a few hours, we landed in Bamako, the capital of Mali. At last, I felt I belonged. This was my homeland and I felt safe. The moment we left the airport we were surrounded by people. We were tourists and everyone wanted to win us as customers. I picked a kind-looking boy out of the crowd and asked him if he knew my father, Amidou Makhawa from Gaya. He said yes, his family knew him very well and I should not worry. He called us a trustworthy taxi driver and told him to take us to the bus for Ségou and put us on it. When we reached Ségou, I asked for the German businessman and we were taken to him. This man was one of the few people who had followed my story from the beginning, but I thought he welcomed us quite coolly.

In Ségou, we went to the market and were immediately surrounded by all the traders! Each of them wanted to make us a special offer. I was familiar with this tactic and knew that we had to be careful. We did not know where we were or where to go, but suddenly, a young man emerged from the crowd. We trusted him and he led us away from the market towards the River Niger. It was not as clean and tidy as in Germany, but we walked and talked and had a good time. Oliver and Uwe did not speak French so they could not talk to the locals, but they managed to communicate using their hands and feet and enjoyed themselves too. To thank the young man who had helped us, Oliver gave him a massage. I shared my candies with the children we met. They were really happy and started to sing and dance.

After a few days in Ségou, Oliver fell seriously ill. He hadn't done his last vaccination against hepatitis A. We had taken the vaccine with us, but when we came to use it, we discovered that there was no syringe in the box. His fever rocketed up to more than 40°C. He was vomiting a lot and had bad diarrhea for hours. I thought he was going to die. We called a doctor, but no one came. We had to stop the fever rising. But how? I decided to fight the fever with ice. I went to the kitchen, found some ice and wrapped it in a towel. I put it on his feet first to bring the heat down gently, then I slowly moved up to calm his heart. All the time, I was praying please do not let him die! I even said out loud, "No one dies with me." I worked on Oliver's body all day and ended up falling asleep in the middle of the night. I do not know how long I had been asleep when a faint voice woke me up: "Hawa, wake up!" I started putting ice on his body again and at last his temperature began to drop, and his heart started beating more calmly. Finally, he fell into a deep sleep. When I felt that he was no longer in danger, I was able to sleep myself.

The next morning, very early, the doctor suddenly arrived. I was angry with him. I told him he was not serious, but he just said he had been far away in a village and it had taken a long time to reach us. He examined Oliver and found nothing. He charged us 250 euros. All that money gone for nothing. We were very angry with this man for taking advantage of our desperate situation. What would have happened to people who did not have any money? Would he not have come at all? Would he have let them die? We went to the hospital. It was a very dirty place. The machines were rusty, and it was scary to be treated there, but we had no choice. They did a blood test, but they did not find anything either.

Little by little, Oliver started to feel better and he regained his strength enough to continue the journey to Gaya. He looked skinny, but he was fine.

Gaya is a big city and I did not have an address for my family, so I said to a taxi driver: "I am Hawa Makhawa, the daughter of Amidou Makhawa. Could you bring me home?" The man replied, "I know your father and I am also your neighbor. Let me bring you home." And indeed, he took us straight to the house. Outside, just like the other time, the first person I saw was my little sister, Adisa. Our eyes met, we recognized each other, and we started to cry. She opened the door so I could kiss her and then she yelled, "Hawa-Khawa is here!"

I went straight into the house to meet my mother, but she was very cold. She said, "Why are you crying? Stop crying now." Oliver and I were shocked by so much indifference. My father seemed very happy. He spoke to me, but eventually asked me for money and when I gave him some, we did not see him again for two weeks! He bought gasoline for his motorcycle, left the house very early in the morning and only came back at night.

One by one, my other brothers and sisters arrived. My big brother Yusuf gave me a necklace as a gift, and then he wanted his gift in return – money of course. I gave him a little and he also disappeared. My big sister told me she had to travel, and she needed money. I gave her some too and she did not reappear the whole time we were there. I was sad about this and Oliver could see why. Some days later, a family member stole Uwe's money. When we saw that we were not welcome, we wanted to leave, but my older brother Kouami convinced us to stay. He was the only one who welcomed us properly. He greeted us in a friendly way and killed a sheep in our honor. This is the greatest respect someone can show you in Africa. Kouami had his own room in my parents' house and he shared it with us. By now he was married and had a sweet little son and his wife was heavily pregnant again.

One day, my brother Madu borrowed Oliver's watch and when I wanted to have it back, he tried to slap me. When Oliver saw what he was about to do, he jumped in front of him and said, "Don't you ever touch her!" It was difficult for Oliver to understand why my family treated me the way they did. They treated me with no respect, as if I was just a bank, and he hated them for it. My mother did soften a little eventually. She made me a *boubou*. Although I ended up paying for it, I thought this gesture was better than nothing.

We stayed in Gaya for two weeks. My Aunt Niara did not live in the family home anymore because my family had thrown her out. She was living with a very nice Christian family some distance away, but we visited her as often as we could. When she held me, I felt as safe as I had when she used to cuddle me as a child. Oliver was very fond of her too. Unfortunately, she was already very old, and we knew that she would not live much longer. She apologized to me for the mistreatment and sexual abuse that I'd suffered as a small child and she continued to tell me that God had great plans for me and that I should stop being angry with him and he would look after me. She said she would pray for me as long as she lived. Niara and Kouami were the only people I was sorry to say goodbye to when we left Mali this time. Deep inside me, I knew that it was the last time I would see Niara and that I would never return to Gaya.

Oliver fell seriously ill when we got back to Germany. He had to stay in hospital for several days and he lost a lot of weight. Eventually, the doctors discovered he had hepatitis A and malaria, and worms in his stomach. They told him he was very fortunate that I had reacted the way I did – the ice had saved his life. He planned to become a doctor later, so he put it all down to experience! Uwe was the only one of the three of us who didn't fall ill in Mali. Oliver and I had made fun of him for taking his homeopathic medicine, which he said would strengthen his immune system, but maybe it did work after all.

My own physical and mental health deteriorated when we got back. I had gone to Gaya hoping to feel the love of my family, but I had not found it. Why were they not interested in me? It is impossible for a child to accept that its parents do not like it. I felt as if I was falling into a bottomless hole. I was thinking, "Who's going to pick me up? What's waiting for me at the bottom?" I was empty, without feeling or pleasure in life and could not find the strength to go on. As soon as I let myself go, pain entered my body and paralyzed me. My belly kept churning. It said to me, "I am trying to digest this pain! And sometimes it hurts when you want to turn a bad feeling into a good one. Be patient, do not worry!" My heart told me, "This pain is too heavy for me. I do not know how to bring light into this darkness." My mind said, "Forget it! There is no hope for us; it's easier to give up!" I could not get out of the hole I had fallen into. I dragged myself through each day but could not concentrate on anything. Nothing made sense anymore. My stomachaches were getting stronger, especially after eating, and I noticed a lump there too. I went to the doctor, who told me I had a hernia and that I needed to have an operation. I went to Oliver's local hospital so that he could take care of me. The operation went well, and I recovered quickly, but I had to go back to the hospital a few weeks after the operation because the hernia reappeared. Even the doctor was speechless about that.

Oliver's mother was also worried about me and one day she sent me to see a shaman from Nepal. She said that what the shaman said always turned out to be right. In my despair, I agreed. One of the methods the shaman used was a pulse reading. After he'd read my pulse, he performed a ritual for me. I felt very well when he did that and even had the impression that something inside me got better afterwards. The shaman told me that the nagas – snakes that inhabit the "underworld" – were interfering in my body and that if I did not do something about them, they would soon attack my heart and I would die. He also claimed that my disability was not innate, but that it had been inflicted on me by my family in Africa and could be undone! In a way, he was right. The naga theory explained my scars. I now had nine scars from my feet up to my belly and, since my last operation in the abdominal area, I had been aware that it was not far from there to my heart. I had also always had the feeling that my heart would stop beating one day. I used to say to Oliver that one morning I would not wake up because my heart would have stopped beating. I did not yet understand the part about my family. It was too much for me to take in at the time. That night, I dreamed I was being chased by snakes. I ran as fast as I could, but in the end, I was still bitten by them and died.

CHAPTER 26

A higher power

The yellow dog: What were your own beliefs?

I have always known that nothing on this Earth happens without a reason. There are no coincidences. I am sure of this because it cannot be by chance that I have to lead such a life. My supreme commandments are not to steal, not to lie or to injure others, not to kill, to see only the good in everything at all times. And never to question God. OK, that last one was a joke.

I have always had a very strong connection to something spiritual, especially as a child and teenager. For me, that was normal, and I thought everyone had the same connection. I often knew things before they happened, and I said things to people I could not really have known. But in Germany this made some people anxious, so I decided not to talk about it. However, I always saw pictures. I sensed people, environments and situations very clearly and I dreamed of some events in advance. Something seemed to be communicating with me.

At the same time, I had to work to find my own place in this society. I tried to be normal, to go the way everyone else seemed to be going. But society did not see me as normal. I am dark-skinned and disabled and I don't have a conventional CV. I don't fit the standard! And that's without the bad experiences from my past that kept popping out. It was too much. Wherever I went, I was always the only dark-skinned, disabled person there. Whatever I did, I could feel everyone's eyes on me. People were always watching me and asking strange questions. And women often appeared to be jealous of me, although I could never work out why. At that time, I wanted to hide. Strangers were always talking about me to my friends, even when I was there. They couldn't believe that I could speak German or that my friends were not my nurses or siblings. They wanted to know where I came from and why I was in a wheelchair.

I was very sensitive, and sometimes I thought I was imagining things. One time, in the tram, I noticed a man who kept looking at me and I sensed that his intentions were not good. I somehow knew that he would get off at the next stop and that before he got off, he would ask me if I wanted to get out too. Sure enough, he suddenly stood up and, just before he got out, he asked me if I was getting off. I said no and was very relieved. I was sure something bad would have come of it. I have had lots of situations like that. Oliver had a habit of losing things and if he called me, I always knew where they were. And I always knew whether or not he was OK.

At night, pictures from the past kept coming to the surface and I couldn't sleep. My self-esteem plummeted. For the first time, I saw myself as a victim and I felt betrayed by life, abused and mistreated. Even though these things had happened years ago, I was unable to pick myself back up. I told Oliver that my illness was getting worse, as the doctors had predicted. I could feel it all over my body. My elementary force was dwindling. Oliver tried to give me courage. He told me I was the strongest woman he knew and that the doctors were mistaken. I took his words to heart and managed to pull myself together, but not for long. I watched my condition becoming more critical but was powerless to change it. I felt that my heart would simply stop beating if I carried on like this. But what had I done to make my condition worse? I was just trying to live a normal life like everyone else.

The only time I managed to relax was when I was being creative. I could never settle on one activity, so I did everything I enjoyed: painting, sewing, working with clay and wood and handicrafts. I gave my creations away with pleasure, because I love to make others happy too.

But the older I became, the more pressure I had in my mind. For a while after I ran away from Frank, I thought I would be able to stop focusing on survival. But now I was fighting for my existence and my place in the world and in society. My expectations and desires grew, but there seemed to be no way for me to feel better. I was trapped in my own golden cage and I couldn't find a way out by myself. I had no family around, I could not expect my friends to feel responsible for me, and to the authorities I was just a number. If I did not do something myself, at some point my light would be extinguished.

Darkness was spreading through my life. My courage was gone and my thoughts were more pessimistic than ever before. That is how my health had worsened: from migraines to heart rhythm disorder to pulmonary embolism to hernia surgery. The doctors told me that my symptoms were psychosomatic or suggested that I might have brought a disease back from Africa. I was referred to the Institute of Tropical Medicine several times, but they did not find anything suspicious. Later, they suspected depression and prescribed medication. The drugs made me even more drowsy and I could not concentrate on anything anymore. At that point I stopped taking them. I knew I did not have depression. It was just that the symptoms were similar.

People close to me did everything they could to bring back the real, joyful Hawa, but nothing helped. Even at school my teachers saw that I had changed and that my thoughts were somewhere else. I realized that in the course of my life I had built a thick wall around me. Somehow, though, I had forgotten to install a door, so I would need help getting out. However, there are not many people who deal with the special material my wall is made of.

CHAPTER 27

Healing

The Yellow dog: Who did you find to help you?

One morning, shortly after waking up, I saw a man in my mind's eye and I knew that I would find him soon. That evening, two friends came over and gave me a list of names of psychologists, because they were worried about me. I glanced down the list and the name Dr. Sorgenlos jumped out at me. I knew immediately that he was the one! I called him, but he said it would be a year before he had a space, so I hung up. After thinking for a bit, I decided to make that appointment for a year's time. So, I called the doctor back. This time, he said he had an appointment available in six months and I said I would take it. He said if I was desperate, I should see his colleague. He gave me her number and I made an appointment with her, but it was clear the moment I arrived that it was not going to be the right place for me: The steps and stairs were too steep and dangerous, even with my helpers. Moreover, the therapist and I were not on the same wavelength. She did not take me seriously and criticized me a lot. When I got home, I called Dr. Sorgenlos again and told him about my bad experience with his colleague. All of a sudden, he said that he had a cancellation in fourteen days' time and I could have the appointment. Finally, at the age of twenty-four, I was happy and full of hope.

I had been sent to see a psychologist once as a child but back then I was not able to talk about my experiences and I kept steering the conversation to the psychologist instead. I was quite skillful at it. Most people want to be listened to and I always listen attentively. So I learned a lot about the psychologist and she learned very little about me. When she realized what was happening, she was ashamed and did not want to treat me anymore.

This time, though, I was older and ready to talk. When I started telling Dr. Sorgenlos my story, he turned pale and almost fell off his chair. I stopped talking then because I thought he didn't believe me, but he said he was simply amazed that I was still alive and looking so well. He said that normally, someone who had been through what I had experienced would have died. And if not, they would be homeless, addicted to drugs and very thin. I was actually very thin because I was vomiting nearly every day. Dr. Sorgenlos believed my story. He explained that I was badly traumatized. He said my heart was under a huge amount of stress – like a deer hunted by a lion in the wilderness. The deer smells the danger and instinctively starts to run. Its heart beats fast and its entire organism gears up, because it is all about survival. When the deer has escaped and is safe again, its heartbeat returns to normal and everything calms down again. Once the danger is over, it starts to graze. However, if it were to remain in that state of existential fear, it would soon die of cardiac arrest.

In really dangerous situations, we have three options: fight, flight or feign death. To some degree we lose the feeling in our body so as to protect ourselves from impending pain. It's as if our soul splits. This is a parasympathetic response, part of the vegetative nervous system that reports danger to the brain. The brain then sends out chemical substances that allow us to survive in that moment. It is an ancient mechanism that we have inherited from our ancestors. Excess energy that is not discharged from the body after a traumatic experience becomes stuck in the nervous system and has a devastating effect on body and mind. In this state we are highly sensitive to our surroundings and people around us. We note gestures, smells, voices, weather and sounds so that we can assess the situation quickly and be ready to react. I have been in survival mode all my life.

Dr. Sorgenlos said it was normal for traumatized children to be highly sensitive to their surroundings and fellow human beings. He told me that my flashbacks – the pictures that kept going around in my head and which stopped me from falling asleep at night or relaxing during the day – were another normal symptom because my brain did not know yet that the danger was past. For the first time I felt I was in the right place. I felt this man would be able to help me, and – above all – I realized I was not crazy.

Dr. Sorgenlos practices Eye Movement Desensitization and Reprocessing (EMDR) therapy. EMDR therapy replaces negative experiences with positive ones. I do have positive experiences, but the brain has a habit of forgetting positive events quickly and clinging to the negative ones. Dr. Sorgenlos told me how I could recognize my flashback triggers and replace them with positivity. My triggers can be people, gestures, situations, rumors, sounds, and even weather – anything that can pull me back into trauma.

Dr. Sorgenlos would sit across from me while I searched for a positive memory and feeling. Then I had to follow his finger movements with my eyes. After the treatment, I felt positive and calm and the feeling stayed with me afterwards too. I remember after one treatment I went into town and beamed with joy the whole time. I was just so happy and content. I wondered when I had been this happy in the last few years, but I couldn't remember. My panic attacks became less and less frequent. I didn't mind being watched anymore. I started to enjoy life. Over time I became happier. I learned to meditate, to have a more positive attitude towards myself. I learned to relax my self-made rules.

I was able to process and release the matter of my adoptive parents relatively quickly. I even wanted to take Frank to court to get justice, but found I was too late to bring a case against him. I was disappointed at first, but then I acknowledged that going to court would have brought everything back, rather than lessening my pain.

Through therapy I learned to sleep with a clear mind. In the first few weeks, I just celebrated sleeping! My migraines vanished because my thoughts were no longer circling and the vomiting stopped too. It's only now that I realize how lucky I was not to have suffered more serious damage from all the times Frank hit me on the head. It is a well-known fact that boxers suffer extreme vibrations to the brain every time they are knocked out. I was learning to communicate better with my body and to listen to it. For example, as soon as the trembling started, I said to myself, "Don't be afraid anymore, I'll take care of you now" and then the trembling lessened. If I woke up in the morning and realized it was going to be difficult for me to get up, I would stay lying down because I had learned that that meant a migraine was coming. The art is to react at the body's first warning sign. It was so good to take my life back step by step. I was no longer at the mercy of circumstances but could also say "no". An inner feeling of freedom arose in me; I felt much lighter. My dreams also became more intense, as if my soul wanted to communicate with me. I needed to start developing a deep understanding for life and for myself.

I gave up evening classes and completed a course as a foreign language correspondent instead. I learned how to stop being helpless and powerless. And I realized that my path in this life is different from that of others. In time, my laughter came back. Like a child, I had to get to know myself. Of course, there were still a lot of issues to work through, but now I was a strong woman who could deal with them.

When I realized that until now, I had only been a product of my environment, I decided to take responsibility for my life and make sure that nothing like that could ever happen to me again. For me, the worst thing is to be manipulated and controlled by other people. The one thing I could not forgive my adoptive father for was that he beat me because he thought I was able to walk and was just pretending. For me, these beatings were unforgivable and impossible to let go of. How can an adult man seriously believe that a child can simulate an illness or disability? Why is he violent towards this child instead of loving it? Yes, that thought gnaws at my soul.

Now, after each treatment with Dr. Sorgenlos, my legs would start to tingle. This tingling became more intense. Of course, it was strange at first and I was scared and asked what it was. He said that the nerves were forming. Sometimes there was even a tingling sensation in my head or spine, but it was stronger in my legs. Now I was eager for more. There was a connection there! Ever since I became paralyzed, people have asked if they can pray for me so that someday

I will walk again. All my friends have dreamed at some point that I could walk. In my own dreams, I am always walking or running. It's only when I dream of my families that I am severely disabled and paralyzed. Moreover, ever since I was a child, I have always had a feeling that one day I would walk again. So I started wondering if there might be something to it. What if all these things were a sign to try? I decided to take better care of my legs and my health. Until then, I had dismissed my legs. I can even remember wanting to get rid of them because I didn't see why I should have to drag these lifeless parts of me everywhere. Seeing my legs also reminded me of all the painful experiences I had left behind me. But now I decided to set myself a goal of walking again in this life. There is so much potential in this long-term goal. It is one I can pursue over the next few decades to keep me alive.

I spent a year thinking intensively about my goal. During my research, I discovered that I was not alone in pursuing it. There have been so-called miraculous healings throughout history. The most famous miracle cure is described in the Bible. I was fascinated by it. Why shouldn't I believe it? I had nothing to lose. Don't we say that faith can move mountains? I had survived worse challenges, and I was determined to master this one too. When I reached the point where I was determined to pursue my goal and go after it with everything I had at my disposal, I made a start. It was almost as if I had done this before. During this time, I had intense dreams that were impossible to ignore. It was as if my soul was talking to me. In most of them, I was in my body and I saw my legs fill with light and could tell they were very happy. Deep down, I knew it could work. There is a power outside of us that responds to everything we do or don't do. I could not have survived without this power. I knew I had breathing difficulties and no real connection to my legs. But any journey begins with a single step.

I had no real feeling in my legs. My feet were full of water and painful to the touch. I had bad scoliosis, which meant my back hurt all the time. My organs were displaced, my pelvis tilted and twisted, my right knee was not properly aligned and my foot was twisted inwards. My left hip was stiff and I couldn't feel it anymore. My left leg was generally lifeless and much shorter than my right. My right arm was so weak that I could not even lift a glass of water, and it kept popping out of the socket because my shoulder joint was out of line with my shoulder blade and the muscles that were supposed to hold everything together were very weak. My whole skeleton was crooked.

Since the EMDR had worked for me and had taught me how to reprogram my brain, I wanted to apply this same approach to my legs. This opened up a whole new area of research for me. In Far Eastern medicine, there is a strong belief in reincarnation, chakras, chi, meditation, meridians, etc. So I started to delve into meditation and chakras. It was obvious that my root chakra was completely blocked. My solar plexus chakra was also badly blocked because I had no attachment to my mother. This also explained my constant gastrointestinal problems. My heart chakra was, of course, also blocked because my heart had been broken so often. My sacral chakra was blocked because of the sexual abuse I had suffered as a small child in Africa. My throat chakra was out of balance because I never expressed my opinion. At least the remaining two chakras worked, phew!

The most important rule on this journey was to respect myself and to be honest with myself. If you whitewash over situations, you lie to yourself. I meditated a lot and stimulated my chakras with different fragrances and gemstones. I started to focus on my breathing. I massaged my legs and imagined myself walking along the beach. My entire attention was focused on healing, so that cell and chemical changes could take place. I learned to speak to my inner child and to see where she is. I have read in countless articles that the brain is not able to distinguish between real and unreal emotions and thoughts. This means we can achieve and change a lot simply through our ideas! Since I had been able to walk in my childhood, I was sure that this information was stored somewhere in my body and mind. It was buried deep because I had been busy with survival, but it was there somewhere.

Because my birth family was at the start of my trauma, I had no choice but to deal with these memories. I had made up my mind to be completely honest with myself, no matter how painful it would be. I was looking for my origins and my identity. I remembered that at one point, when I was a small child, I wanted to stop walking, because

I was sure that then nobody would hurt me and that my mother would love me and finally take care of me. Now I asked myself: Why would a child wish for such a thing? I knew that something very bad had happened to me in my childhood in Gaya. My early memories are only fragments, but they keep coming back. I was certain that I must have suffered sexual abuse in some form because sex always made me vomit. Any time I became physically intimate with someone, the nausea would rise.

Today, I know that I was sexually abused at a very young age and that my desire to stop walking came after that. And when I had the vaccination, my immune system was very weak from having to fight to survive for the first time. That's where the anger came from that I felt when I was a child. This experience, which occurred so far back in my past, was still stored in my body. It's called cell memory. The danger is that conditioning can occur if this happens too often. That's why I need an empathic partner who understands my situation and who can give me the time I need. These men are rare, but they do exist.

It took me years to deal with this issue. I talked to Dr. Sorgenlos about it. He took me seriously and was not even surprised. This is something that is known to occur only in women who have been abused in the first three years of their lives. His job was not to put the words and thoughts in my mouth. He said self-knowledge is the key to change. With Dr. Sorgenlos, I started to treat my deep rage using EMDR. Each time, my legs started to tingle more and strong feelings returned to parts of me that used to be numb. I soon realized that I was doing something right and I had to keep going.

I needed to focus more on myself and so, after seven years, I ended my relationship with Oliver. I did not know that it was possible to break up with someone in a nice way, but he understood me and accepted my decision. He is still my best friend and brother. We still call each other regularly and we will always stay in touch. Neither of us will let go of the other in this life. Love is unconditional, and it is possible for men and women to love on different levels. I am grateful to him because without him I would not have known this form of love.

Around this time I came across the Feldenkrais method, a kind of guided movement approach that helps people become more conscious of the body and learn new patterns of movement. The idea is that you can change your sensory perception, feeling and thinking through complex movements. I found a practice close to me run by someone called Bea. Feldenkrais deals with early childhood movements that are stored in our unconscious. The body knows best how to arrange itself and connect to carry out movements with ease in everyday life. Moshé Feldenkrais said, "If you do not make mistakes, you cannot learn."

In the first few years, Bea and I worked only with my upper body, because I did not yet have a connection to my lower extremities. The work on my shoulders made my hips very noticeable. And every physical change, whether large or small, caused my thinking and feelings to change as well. What is so special about Feldenkrais for me is that every inner change is also reflected externally. Only once I had passed this test could I experience movement. I found I had to vomit every time I learned a new movement. My rigid shoulders became more and more flexible and the more stable I became inside, the less I had to vomit. I began to sit in a wheelchair quite differently. My posture was better and more stable. A few times I envisaged quite clearly throwing myself out of the wheelchair and rolling. This always made me laugh out loud. Bea and I realized then that I was about to become more flexible – that I was able to act more flexibly on the outside too. I got to know my body in a new way. The feeling of being disabled diminished and I started to feel healthier.

My body began to communicate more with me. Suddenly, I had an urge to crawl again and I started exploring my apartment on my hands and knees. Crawling for the first time after so many years was strange because it felt so new. To start with, my knees swelled up but, as the swelling went down, they proved much stronger than before and I could stay on my knees without any problems. Later, I felt like sliding. I did that too and felt like a worm as I managed to slither along. Who knew so much could happen in my body? I could feel that my body was grateful for the work.

Soon after that, I wanted to kneel up and then one day I was finally ready to stand up. I had no chair in my apartment to lean on, so Bea lent me one. At home, I used the chair to pull myself up to standing. This was a very unusual sensation for me and incredibly beautiful. My first thought was "Wow, am I big!" I felt like a giant. I couldn't believe it – there was a time when I would have collapsed if I'd tried to stand up. My heart was full of joy and awed that I was part of a miracle.

I felt great and became more self-confident. Bea always said to me that I was like an overripe fruit waiting to be plucked, so small changes were enough to make a big difference. My daily mantra was "I am healed" to develop a pattern of thought. My being was changing for the better and I was rediscovering myself. As my self-esteem grew, I started letting people into my life who liked me and letting go of the people who exploited and manipulated me. I was amazed to see how many negative friends I had accumulated over the years. I had clung onto them even though they were sucking the life out of me. So many times, I was annoyed with myself for not having listened to my gut feeling because it would have saved me a lot of grief. Bea told me I should imagine my body is my house. Since I had gone out and left the door wide open, people from the Taking tribe had moved in. They were not going to disappear just because I suddenly wanted my house back. These people had become accustomed to living in it because there were no rules or limits. My job was to take back my home, send them away and make sure that nothing like that happened again.

CHAPTER 28

Forgiveness

The yellow dog: How did you process the experience with your adopted parents?

One day, I was at a friend's house when my cell phone rang. I answered, and a man I didn't know said, "Just a minute, someone wants to talk to you." Then suddenly Frank was on the other end. He had managed to find my number online through my jewelry business. I froze. I thought I was going to die on the spot. He talked as if nothing had happened and wanted to chat. But I got rid of him and hung up. I couldn't breathe and was hyperventilating. my friends had to reassure me that I was OK.

On the way home, I felt haunted by him. I saw him everywhere. I was the little helpless Hawa all over again. I imagined him waiting for me in the entrance. My heart was racing and I was sweating. Eventually I remembered that I could call the police, and that he had no right to do anything to me. I focused on this thought until I was home. Once I was safely inside, I thought about how I could conquer this fear of Frank once and for all. Dr. Sorgenlos had given me some very good tools and I used them: I breathed deeply in and out, closed my eyes, and imagined Frank was standing in front of me. I tried to locate the parts of my body where these fears were held. They were predominantly in the upper body, neck, shoulders and heart. I breathed deeply into these areas to fill them with love and light.

In my mind's eye, I could see that I had now become much stronger than Frank. Our circumstances had changed. That little weak, helpless child had become a grown woman with a lot of loving and caring friends around her. Every single one of them would protect me from Frank this time. To be afraid of him only meant that I was letting him have power over me so I didn't have to take responsibility. This gave me strength and courage and in my imagination, I reached out to take Frank's hand and I forgave him because that was a way of forgiving myself – forgiving myself for not having been strong enough to defend and protect myself.

After that, I was calm and I slept. That night, I dreamed of Frank. In the dream, I was a child again. I was living with him and he was about to attack me. But it occurred to me in my dream that I was strong now, so the little girl in the dream stood before him and made herself big and said to him, "I am not afraid of you anymore" and then he calmed down and said "Good." I woke up feeling happy and liberated.

A few days later I felt ready to talk to Frank about the past. As an awakening woman, I have the right to know why someone would mistreat a disabled child. First, I prayed for heavenly help so that I would get all the answers to my questions, and then I called him. Frank was actually happy that I had called. I asked him why he had treated me like that and he said he was very sorry for what I had had to go through. He had never actually intended to bring me to Germany, but he did not want to have me on his conscience. Fabienne had taken no responsibility for me at all and there was a civil war raging in Volta. That was hard to hear, but true! He also said he was very sorry that my African family did not want anything to do with me, and he found it hard to believe that my father had requested money for me. I already knew about that from my big brother Kouami, but that was a matter for another day. I was just glad then that Frank had opened up to me. I felt my heart responding in harmony. That phone call really brought me peace. It was about conquering my fears and also recognizing that, without these circumstances, I would not have become the woman I am now. When Frank fell into his old patterns again, I said goodbye and hung up.

I had wanted an apology and now I had one. At last, my fear of Frank had vanished and that was all that mattered. I felt a lot of space in my body.

A positive experience like that can become addictive! So I decided to look for Fabienne and see if I could have a grown-up conversation with her as well. I had only met two inexperienced women in my life so far and they were my birth mother and my adoptive mother – two women from two very different continents. What kind of women *are* they? I could never treat a sick child – my own or someone else's – with hatred. After a long search I found Fabienne on a social network. She was living in America now with a husband and two children (twins) and working as a naturopath. Her life seemed to be perfect, but I thought the fact that this woman was working as a healer was a mockery.

Now that Fabienne was a mother herself, I thought she would have a full understanding of what she had done to me. I wanted to know from her whether she thought it was normal to snatch a sick child from her family and home and leave her in the hands of a violent man. So I wrote her a message and confronted her with her part in the story. Fabienne wrote back saying that she had been young at the time and that the whole thing had been Frank's idea. She said she had nothing to do with it and I should be grateful that I was living in Europe now, instead of with my family in Africa, where there was only poverty.

Soon after I received this message, I got another one saying "Oops, pressed the wrong button" and she deleted me! I could not believe a healer would show such a lack of responsibility for her own actions. For me, Fabienne's behavior is a prime example of denial and irresponsibility. And this was a woman who claimed to heal people? How can someone be so hypocritical? A part of me felt sorry for the poor people who go to her in hope. Another part of me knew that like attracts like. Now I was angry with Fabienne. For the first time in my life I felt I wanted revenge on her. I called my best friend Chloé and together we talked for a long time about what had happened until I calmed down. The main thing was to talk to someone about it and not keep these strong negative thoughts inside me. Once again, I found release and acceptance. In this case, I would have to trust that life itself would provide justice. For the first time in my life, I was developing a deep understanding and compassion for myself.

It is really nice to have a friend like Chloé. I can tell her everything. She is patient and listens to me and will even spend hours on the phone encouraging me. I do the same for her. We motivate each other. There has never been a problem between us and we see each other often. One time, we travelled to Spain together. We went to the beach every day. We were so relaxed! At first, we met a lot of people, but not all of them were well-intentioned. Most of them did not understand why we had come to town on our own. But why shouldn't we? Many people thought Chloé must be my carer, rather than my friend, and others asked us if we were a couple. Eventually, we just kept ourselves to ourselves and had a good vacation. This trip brought us closer together. Chloe lost six kilos pushing me all over town! We discovered a new weight-loss concept: If you want to lose weight, go travelling with someone in a wheelchair!

When I first came up with the idea of walking, it was Chloé's opinion that was decisive for me. She has believed in me all along, and she knows I will make it.

Now, Chloé's daughter Jolie supports me too. I am happy to have a wonderful relationship with them both. It is a beautiful gift. When Jolie talks about me to her friends, she calls me her aunt or her BFF. I know part of the reason she loves me so much is because she feels the strong bond between me and her mother. Jolie has started writing letters to me. I love receiving them and answering them.

CHAPTER 29

Gemstones and crystals

The yellow dog: Did you try any other healing therapies?

I faced lots of challenges during this time, but I saw every challenge as a chance to grow. I thought: Anything that doesn't kill me will make me stronger.

It has not been an easy journey but the moments when I was at my lowest emotionally were the ones that made me stronger – as soon as I learned my lessons from them and took responsibility for myself.

A naturopath told me that the tip of a small rock crystal can heal tissue scars because it has a very strong, purifying vibration. She gave me a crystal and I tried it, because I had nothing to lose. It worked! As if by a miracle, life came back to those areas, on my left hip especially. The doctors I had seen in Germany had told me that dead tissue will always remain dead, but now my tissue was alive! Behind each scar was an emotional and spiritual pain that needed to be dissolved.

Within a few years, my body, mind and soul improved dramatically. As soon as I let go of the past, I started growing. This had nothing to do with faith. It was a natural process, since my focus was now directed solely towards healing. I was experiencing in my own body the power of positive thinking. But I know there is a higher power over us. Without it, none of these changes would be noticeable to me.

During this time, I decided to go self-employed and, since I enjoy expressing myself creatively and love gems and natural materials, I opted for jewelry design. Everyone likes jewelry and it doesn't hurt anyone. When I was offered a room, I opened my jewelry studio and did very well. People loved my artwork and they liked to wear and buy it too. I made unique pieces, since we are all unique. Customers could decide on their own colors, stones, length and closure. Some people gave me heirlooms to turn into beautiful, modern pieces of jewelry.

My work as a jewelry designer was a lot of fun and went well until the landlord died. The new owner kept taking me to court because she wanted to build apartments. I was fighting to stay because I knew it would not be easy to find another wheelchair-accessible space. Eventually, though, I was forced out. But even then, I did not let the set-back get the better of me. Since I had learned to get out of such unpleasant situations faster, I thought that since I didn't know how the shop would survive, I would concentrate on my training. I could certainly get more out of that.

All my therapists soon noticed the strong physical and mental changes in me. They were also seized by curiosity. There was a question in the room: How far would we go if we continued? Friends noticed these positive developments too and rejoiced with me. They encouraged me to keep going.

CHAPTER 30

Doubters

The yellow dog: What about your goal to walk again?

I decided to do even more fitness training. I got in touch with the health insurance company because now we were talking about a realistic possibility that someday I would walk again. I collected all the documents and findings I needed from my various doctors and therapists, and the insurance company approved my request for a fitness rehabilitation program. For the first time in my life, I would be able to have rehab fitness training sessions – although not at my preferred center because it didn't have a contract with the health insurance company. They sent me to a different facility.

I soon realized that I was out of place there. The staff didn't take me seriously and the doctors wanted to re-operatively stiffen all my joints. There was an orthopedic surgeon, supposedly an expert in his field, who made fun of my knees and said to me, "I haven't seen knees like those since the Second World War." He said it would be impossible to walk with them, so they would have to be stiffened. Of course I refused. I was very sad that doctors treating me for the first time were laughing at me and not taking my problems seriously. The neurologist there told me that if I said the word "walk" one more time, he would send me to the psychiatric ward! Most of the nurses also laughed at me. The doctors there tried to tell me that all the doctors and therapists who had been treating me until now had no idea what they were doing and were crazy – like me. Only they themselves knew what they were doing. I was treading on thin ice there and the doctors were gods in white.

I was so unhappy that I started getting sick again, but now I knew I needed to stay true to myself and listen to my feelings. I talked to my insurance company, because doing something that was not working was just a waste of time and money. We agreed on an outpatient rehab arrangement and I was allowed to arrange it myself. Back home, I set up my own training plan and found a very good physiotherapist called Tom and another very good doctor, Dr. Hoffnung, who is also known as the television doctor. He looks beyond the body to the underlying emotional issues. He is a true luminary in his field and people from all over Europe come to him! He has also written several books on fibromyalgia, chronic pain disorders and functional disorders and nutrition. He knows that many ailments can be cured through the right treatment, medications, diet and positive thinking. Physical ailments are in most cases associated with mental problems.

Dr. Hoffnung immediately noticed my achievements and my willpower. In his practice I use the Alter G, an anti-gravity treadmill. This machine has a very high success rate. It deals with intuitive gait patterns. My legs started getting stronger and so did my immune system. Dr. Hoffnung's colleagues, who could see my successes, encouraged me to continue with the training. I also made very good progress with my physiotherapy sessions and Tom became my mentor. He encouraged me to keep going whenever I wanted to give up. Now I was slowly building muscle and trying to get my nerves to connect to my brain.

My feet were changing, too. I had developed a healthy relationship with my body. In all this time I never had a relapse. Sometimes my body ached, but these pains were different. Positive aches come before big changes. Sometimes cell changes have to express themselves in pain before they eventually disappear completely. I also had sore muscles as the new muscle was developing, but I never had the same pain twice – clearly, the underlying emotional issues were always different too. My right shoulder was now stronger as well and I could lift a glass of water with my right hand.

This situation didn't last though. The dismissive doctor at the first rehabilitation center had written in my final report that my desire to walk was completely unrealistic. As a result, my health insurance company told me I had to stop the physiotherapy. They were more convinced by a rehab doctor who didn't know me than by the facts. They ignored my usual doctors, therapists and the videos I sent, even though they all demonstrated my success. The insurance company even threatened my regular doctor and banned him from giving me any more prescriptions! They bullied Tom and accused me of making money from the prescriptions.

This accusation was incredibly hurtful, especially when I could prove that I had made a huge amount of progress with the treatment. This fight with the insurance company sapped all my strength. I was incredibly disappointed that they weren't taking me seriously and giving me the support I needed. Instead of helping me, they wanted me to stay home and become even sicker! In the end I was forced to switch insurance companies.

I started searching for an intensive training program for young disabled people who have not given up. For people who want to try to overcome their disability, whether it delivers results or not – because the path is the goal. I eventually found a facility in the USA and kind friends arranged for me to go there. This rehab clinic was completely different from the one in Germany. It specializes in training people with disabilities and has developed a special approach to connect nerves with the brain. I trained for two or three hours every day there and saw real benefits. The first hour was the most exhausting, because I had to establish the nerve connection. I would think of a movement, for example turning my foot from side to side. The command comes from the brain and is then passed on through the nerve pathways to the foot. This requires repetition. In the beginning, the movement only happened in my head. The therapist stimulated the nerve pathways by simply tapping my leg. At some point, my foot moved by itself and without effort. I grinned – now I knew I was on the right path. It meant the effort was worthwhile. The second hour was about building up the muscles. For this we used fitness equipment. One of my highlights was when I could cycle on the spin bike! I couldn't believe I was doing this alone. I kept asking where the motor was, and they always replied, "No, it's not electric. That's you". Learning to bend my legs was also a nice surprise and my legs became stronger every time. I loved going there every day. The exercises continued until the trainer thought I was ready to walk. They had a walker – a contraption that they strapped me into with a button to move it up and down. Using the walker, they straightened me up and I started walking on my own. My heart jumped for joy. Amazing! I couldn't believe I was walking without braces. Of course, it was exhausting, but at the same time exhilarating. All the work was worth it. I was shaken with humility. Isn't life wonderful?

Of course, clean, healthy eating is also very important. I have always relied on my body for that, because it knows best what and how much it needs. My portions became bigger and bigger. To be honest, I was always hungry because I was obviously using more energy than I could take in. My body was changing and my legs were thickening. I went up a dress size. There was nothing to stop these changes taking place because I had no everyday stress there and my focus was only on training. At the same time, I noticed how my self-confidence was growing. Many of my fears and worries simply disappeared and I could see myself as part of the whole. I have rarely felt such a deep connection to myself. I felt as if I had been born anew and my intuition also became more fine-tuned, leading me to the right people, places and situations, which had a lasting, positive impact on my life.

While I was in America, I also saw a chiropractor. He had been recommended to me by several people and was very sensitive. He knew what he was doing and his treatments were gentle. He helped me correct my spine and pelvis. He also worked on healing the soul, and I am sure that this treatment accelerated my walking progress. He did meditation exercises with me and, since he had been adopted too, he understood my situation. He encouraged me to forgive my mother so that I could make better progress in my healing. I always felt tired after the treatment, so I knew it was having a positive effect on my soul. The next day, my training felt easier and more intensive. My spine also changed a lot during this time.

My coaches were enthusiastic about these rapid achievements and changes but, unfortunately, my time there was far too short. I knew the end was coming and I wished I could stay there longer. It was with a heavy heart that I said goodbye to my trainers and friends. But I had made the most of my time there. I had met some amazing people and I was walking! In Germany we would be able build on my progress.

I was able to get a walker from the health insurance company and I took it with me to Tom so that we could continue with the walking practice. Considering how much slower training programs are in Germany, with fewer prescribed therapy courses, I made very good progress.

In the meantime, my extreme scoliosis was nearly gone and my pelvis was constantly changing, giving me greater stability. My left leg was getting stronger all time. I was also stronger mentally than I had ever thought possible. The trip to America had given me more that I imagined. I was happier and more satisfied, and grateful that my life had taken such a beautiful turn for the better.

CHAPTER 31

Waves

The yellow dog: How did you discover adaptive surfing?

In the training center in America I met an older man called Andrew. He lives alone and practices adaptive surfing. He has a trailer and is very self-sufficient. Andrew became my new role model. One day he asked if I wanted to try adaptive surfing. It was a revelation: As soon as I was in the water with the board, I fell in love with the sport. I was not afraid. Being in the ocean felt like regaining a deep confidence in life, in the waves and in myself. It was like being back in Volta. A new birth! I would love to find that confidence on land too because I need it to walk, but that is much more difficult.

When I discovered the world of surfing, I met other people with disabilities, and the able-bodied people who help them get into the water. This kind of solidarity was new to me. The people without disabilities were touched that they had the opportunity to help. Here, disability was no longer at the center of people's lives – it was the love of surfing that brought them together.

I met lots of other wonderful people there – strangers who helped me and spent time with me without trying to take advantage of me. After training, I went to a Christian church and I met some wonderful people there too. I do not practice any religion, but I believe that there is something above us, an extraordinary force. In that church, I realized that it was possible to be drawn together by faith. It was the first time I had found a church that respected people, without trying to control them or get involved in their private lives. At least that was my impression. I was touched by their simple, warm welcome. They took care of me and showed me the city. At Christmas they invited me to their houses and gave me gifts, including my first waterproof camera! I even made a friend in the supermarket: Violetta, a very nice, natural woman. One day, the training center was organizing a gala and Violetta helped me find a beautiful dress and her daughter-in-law came and did my hair and make-up.

I also made a friend called Chuck. He worked for Uber and came to the training center to pick me up one day. I liked him and his dog "Charlie" right away and we became friends on that first trip. Chuck became my "grandfather". He took me everywhere and watched over me. We had some amazing conversations. He also witnessed my physical changes as time went on and was happy for me. He remains very close to my heart.

It was the Soul-Surfer dream, with all the clichés of sun, beach, surfing and kind people. I felt I had found one of life's treasures. Throughout my time there I felt protected by an unseen hand. It seemed to me that time came to a standstill there. I had seldom encountered so much love and my heart was moved. I did meet some bad people too, but they are no longer in my focus. Those kinds of people are everywhere. In California I made some friends for life.

I came back to Germany with a lot of strength and inspiration. I found a surf school in a small village in southern France that agreed to train me. This school also specializes in adaptive surfing. Every time I come back from surfing, my gait pattern improves as my unconscious muscles are stimulated, and my self-confidence increases. I now feel like at home in the surf community. It is a pity that I have no opportunities to do this sport in Germany.

My biggest highlight was the world championship. My French coach, Jule, encouraged me to take part and I managed to come fourth in my first competition. I have been so inspired by adaptive surfing that I have even started to write about it. I have also started to share my exercises on social media to encourage others with disabilities to work on their body, and to make them understand that even if the goal of walking may seem unrealistic to others, it is an important path to take for oneself and for one's self-esteem.

I have learned that it is vital to have a good coach, therapist and doctors, and there needs to be real teamwork between them – this is the best gift they can give each other. The results come with time and it takes a lot of willpower to train every day and to change one's view of life. You also need to eat and to sleep well, because it is during sleep that the body heals. And you need positive people around you to lift you up.

CHAPTER 32

Icebergs

The yellow dog: What are you working on now?

To reach a better understanding of my family of origin and to get answers to my questions, I went to a healing practitioner called Anne. Anne was recommended to me because she specializes in Psychology ofVision, a healing model. Psychology ofVision is a model of emotional intelligence that leads to a deeper awareness of our self and our relationships through our hearts, spirituality and psychology.

Using this model, I worked through some family processes. I looked deep under the iceberg. The aim is to take responsibility for oneself and to let go in love. Anne always created a safe atmosphere to help us open up. We used role play, with people taking on positive and negative roles to deal with problems. The idea is to try to understand and solve everything with the spirit. Anne was understanding when our egos tried to take charge because this part of us is trained to take control in all areas. Avoiding dealing with this shadow self is only human. When we ignore these aspects, we lie to ourselves and look for other people to blame, thinking it will make us feel better. It is difficult to accept that we are part of the problem rather than blaming things on an external culprit.

Unfortunately, there is no school that can teach us how to communicate with our soul because we all have different issues and different talents. Since half our DNA comes from our mother and the other half from our father, we also carry their ancestral dynamics inside ourselves. Unprocessed conflicts shape us and need to be dissolved. Each conflict also hides a gift. But since the emotional pain behind the conflict is too great, we refuse to look at it and the ego takes control. But it is the heart's task, not the ego's, to dissolve these conflicts.

The other participants found some of my processes challenging because African energy is not like European energy. I understood during these sessions that my relatives in Africa are themselves prisoners and that they only passed on what they had learned from their parents. And we will continue to pass down what we've received from them. This is called ancestor dynamics. As an example, my parents had to reject me because I was the only child who reflected these inner pains and split parts back at them. I overwhelmed them on an emotional level. If their hearts had been open, they would have taken care of me. In order not to betray my parents, I chose adoptive parents who reflected this rejection repeatedly. At the heart level, I quickly understood that I am also a creator and that there are no coincidences.

The Earth is the only planet on which the soul can manifest itself in a body in order to evolve. This is my theory. Since my soul suffers greatly and has many unprocessed issues, the only way it can manifest this clearly is through my body. There was a deep issue hidden behind every illness and suffering. In this world of duality, there were certain issues I did not come across. I also understood that I needed all of the diseases and tragedies that existed in my family in order to dissolve the negative ancestor dynamics and to grow. I understood that I am not a product of my environment and that I can only take responsibility for myself. Since my family was far away and I did not really know them, my soul had to be where I could create situations and find people that would confront me with these issues.

By forgiving my family, I forgive myself. The sooner I release this negativity, the faster I can be positively healed. After each release, my legs started to tingle again, and my damaged nerves sent signals to my equally damaged muscle groups, which gave me a sense of physical health and vigor. As my charisma changed, I recognized the positive impact on my fellow human beings. I could feel all over my body how happy my soul was that I was doing this work. Body, mind and soul are connected, and healing takes place at all levels. Everything in life aspires to a balance.

I found this self-work strenuous. I wanted to recognize my own patterns and inner resistances so I could cope with challenges better. I also understood that I wanted to work on these difficult subjects for my soul – in order to be able to realize myself and escape from the bondage of the victim role, which requires a perpetrator.

After I had managed to let go of my family and other people, I began to wage these conflicts with God and then with myself. This is also quite normal. As I said, there is a part of me that will keep trying to portray itself as a victim. Because of my difficult path in life, I was forced to identify my issues and work on them. This is a process I will keep working through and I will keep finding new issues.

I have found that life always brings me people to help me with energy work. Yasmine was one of them. She was born in Turkey and as a child she could see into the future. In her homeland, people often came to her to ask about their future and what they could do to solve their problems. She came to Germany as a young adult. Even with me, she could see a lot of things that she wouldn‘t have been able to know otherwise. She confirmed that most of the blockages in my system come from my birth family. She was able to dissolve many of them through foot massages. Her hands became quite hot when she did this and I could feel it working. At the moment, she is helping me from a distance using light work and rituals to help my legs connect more with my body. Since travelling to Tibet, her work has become even stronger and more intense and she has higher vibrations. Whenever she works with me, I feel my body hurting as if something is changing. Yasemine always says that my inner willpower accelerates these processes even more. When I went to my physiotherapy sessions, Tom noticed that I suddenly had a different body awareness and that my gait had improved. I loved seeing the questioning look on his face!

I also work with Txika from France. Txika is the only other person I have met who has lived in Gaya. She gives me reiki treatments from a distance once a week and it works. Every time we are connected, my heartbeat changes and I feel calmness spreading through me. My body relaxes quickly and when she starts I feel an extreme heat all over my body. Sometimes I feel like a heater! She feels it too, so she knows I am present. This work is important to my soul and I have stopped questioning it.

There are things I know now that I didn't know before:

- I don't have polio. If I did, all this progress would not be possible.
- The vaccination I was given was called Quinimax and was against malaria. I did not have the polio vaccine.
- Medically, there is no explanation for my progress.
- I don't know how old I am. The age on my documents is not my real age.
- I come from a family that tends to use black magic.
- I was meant to be sacrificed, but I survived.

Thank you for your visit, my dear friend. My soul feels free now and relief is spreading through me. Talking to you about all of this has shown me that there is no longer any reason to remain silent about things that constitute abuse and mistreatment, especially towards children. We need to release emotional pain from every cell in the body so that we can discover and see our true core. This is what generates hope.

CHAPTER 33

My kingdom

The yellow dog: Thank you for telling me your story.

When I tell my story, I tell it as if it was someone else's. But these are not things that happened to someone else. They happened to me. I try not to hold hatred or bear grudges. I seek peace but before I can find it, I have to win back my kingdom – the one that was stolen from me. I am the only one who knows the extent of this kingdom. I listen to the echoes inside me from the past. I listen, and I try not to let go of a single scrap. I do not know all its secrets. Some of them still elude me but I know in my heart that I have to try to understand them if I want to make myself whole.

The history and geography of my kingdom are intimately linked. The rugged landscape that is my body is the living proof. It is my story that it tells, and also the geography of all the places I have been, of everything I've endured. Sometimes I feel ashamed – ashamed of my life, of what happened to me. I feel like an old turtle.

When I think of my body, I see it as a devastated land, an invaded country that my willpower is rebuilding little by little. It is a simple and beautiful land. Others can cross it, violate it, try to discover its most intimate passages, but only I have the key. Knowledge of this territory leads to me. It is a conquest that cannot be achieved with force. Violence is no longer permitted on these shores. Only my willpower has held this land together all these years.

In my kingdom, the motto is: Never give up. Always focus on what is important. Keep your eyes on the sun ahead.

We each have to follow our own path. We have to create our own way. If you dream of flying, then fly! If you find the light that dances in you, it will illuminate your way. Let's see where your path will take you.

My story is not over yet. The journey still goes on, but more than half of it is behind me, so I can manage the rest as well, right?

Useful links

www.aminaaminger.com

www.emdria.org more information about EMDR therapy

www.psychologyofvision.com the international page of Psychology ofVision

www.feldenkrais.com Feldenkrais method

www.irieocean.com Blog about Adaptive Surfing

www.lehena.com Surf School also for Adaptive Surfing

POSTSCRIPT

My birth family

The yellow dog: What can you tell me about your aunt and siblings?

Niara, my lovely aunt

My aunt Niara lived with us when I was a little girl in Gaya and cared for me. She had studied in France and married a Frenchman, but they did not have any children and her husband died in an accident. After the death of her husband and her father, she decided to return to Gaya and work as a nurse. It was because of her that the first hospital was built in the city, and she worked there.

Everyone knew Niara. She owned nothing apart from the clothes she wore. She gave everything away. When Frank, my adoptive father visited her, she always wanted to serve him good German beer. She was a psychic – she could see the future using a cowrie shell – and this gift earned her some money. When I became ill, she treated me like a daughter. She was the one who fed me, dressed me, and gave me my first wheelchair. She used to carry me on her back. I slept next to her and she protected me. She was already old then and her eyesight was failing. I used to thread her needle for her when she was sewing.

My aunt Niara was the good fairy of the family, and all the children loved her! She told me that children are the happiness of the world. She always treated us well, and she always had candies for us. Whenever I came back to Gaya, I would throw myself into her arms, stocking up on all the love I needed to survive until the next time. Now, when I feel lonely, I talk to her. I think she watches over me and I believe she sends me health and vitality. She was a good soul. I'd like to be like her, and I want her to be proud of me.

The year before Niara's death, when I was in Gaya, she asked me how many years I thought she had left to live. My intuition told me that she had only one year left, but I said, "five" and she smiled and told me that was a nice thing to say. She too knew that she had only one year left. The following year I did not want to return to Gaya because I was sure she would die when I got there. Since I did not know how to deal with this situation, I went to Guadeloupe with a friend instead. The day I came back, I woke up at 5 in the morning knowing that my father would call me to announce Niara's death. When he did, I was not surprised, and he could not understand my reaction because he knew how much I loved Niara. I had prepared myself though and I thought she was better off in heaven, where she would no longer be suffering. I believed she would guide my way.

Niara's death touched me deeply. Since she died, I have been looking for my place in the family. When I told my psychoanalyst that something was wrong because my favorite aunt had just died and I was not crying, he said that we all have our own way of mourning, and that it is not obligatory to cry. Now I do not want to go back to Gaya, because she is no longer there to greet me.

Kouami

My big brother Kouami also took care of me when I became ill. He was everything to me! Between them, Kouami and Niara gave me all the affection I needed to live. Kouami always made me laugh and he played with me a lot. I remember one day after my illness, when I could no longer walk, I started exploring – crawling around the courtyard on my own. Kouami gave me some food. The rooster saw it and wanted his share but I was very hungry so I refused to give him any. The rooster attacked me and Kouami came and took him away, but from that moment on, it was war between the bird and me and I still have a scar from where he attacked me.

Kouami was always full of ideas. My adoptive father taught him how to weld. At the time, Kouami was the only person in Gaya to start a business with a soldering machine. He planted trees in the neighborhood and made sure they were well protected, so that the goats would not eat them. One day, out of wickedness, my father took a hammer and destroyed all the plants. He told me that story with a sad voice. My mother broke my brother's heart because she refused to let him marry his first love. She was a pretty girl and they were very much in love, but my mother refused because the girl did not have the same blood as our family. Kouami eventually married more than once and had several children.

When I was in Germany, I wanted Kouami to help me build a house for my little sisters. Oliver and I sent Kouami a little money every month, but when I asked him for the pictures, he got angry. I understood then that he had used the money for something else. One day he told me that if I did not send him a thousand euros he would go to jail. Later, he called and told me that he was in prison, but I could hear the noise of the cars on the street. I think he changed because he was disappointed with life and gradually became embittered. But it makes me very sad that he wants to take advantage of me. Nevertheless, he is still my beloved brother and I understand the circumstances that made him like this.

Zola

My big sister Zola was very beautiful when she was young, and very vain. She was always walking around with a mirror. All she thought about was her looks, her clothes and her hair. She was always jealous of me though. When I came back to Gaya as a teenager, I gave her my money and my passport to look after, but soon afterwards she said she only had the passport and did not know who had taken the money. This happened three times. I trusted her and I did not want to believe that my own sister was stealing from me. The third time, my brothers looked for the money everywhere with me, but we did not find it. Then Kouami confessed that he knew that Zola had taken my money, and that he was ashamed about it. When I was with her, she always cheated to get money. If we went to the market, for example, the prices automatically went up... I am not in contact with her, but I heard that she is married and that she takes care of her children. Of course, I still love her and forgive her.

Yusuf

My big brother Yusuf was the handsome guy in the family. When he came with me to Volta, he would disappear for hours at a time, sometimes even all night long, because he was chasing girls (or because the girls were chasing him). People often mixed the two of us up because we looked very similar then, despite the age gap, and I wore my hair very short.

During my second trip to Gaya with Frank, Yusuf asked me why I was not married. I asked him why I should get married and he told me that he was going to find me a husband and that, because he was my big brother, I would have to obey him. I told him that if he came to fetch me from Germany to get married, I would go with him. Of course, I knew there was no way he could come to Germany to fetch me. Kouami, who was listening to our conversation, laughed.

Yusuf is married now. He also calls me from time to time, but only to ask me to send him money. Little by little, I am starting to understand their language!

Madu

I do not know if I really want to talk about this brother. He is the only one who still makes me angry when I think about what he did and said. One day he called me to ask me for money and I refused. He said I had a duty to send him money because it was thanks to him that I was in Germany. When I laughed, he became angry and insulted me. He said he would get a witch to cast a spell to make me die. Fortunately, I do not believe that kind of superstitious nonsense and I made fun of him. Since that day, I have cut off all contact with Madu. It makes me sad because I am trying to have a good relationship with my unknown family.

Adisa

The sister I am very close to is Adisa. She is no more than a year older than me. We may even be twins. When we meet, we do not talk; we cry. Every time I went back to Gaya, I arrived unannounced, and it was always her that I saw first. And we always cried.

Adisa was in a long relationship with a man, but my mother did not agree to them getting married. She found a husband for her – someone she did not know, supposedly a cousin. Adisa did not want to marry this man and started a hunger strike. My mother ended up giving in. But when I was in Germany, I heard that Adisa had been married off to an older, traditional man as a second or third wife, and that was why she was no longer in Gaya. I have had no news since then. If I become rich one day, the first thing I will do is go and pick her up with all her children. We have the right to dream!

Bijan

My little brother Bijan is a year or two younger than me. I was sad when I left him because he was just a baby, and I would have liked to continue playing with him. It was his birth we were celebrating the day things went wrong. But we did not stay together long. He is the most beautiful boy in the family for me and it broke my heart to leave him, because I did not know who was going to take care of him. Moreover, I learned that my other brothers were mean to him because he was shy and did not speak much. Now that he has made his life, he has not changed. We are still in touch and he talks to me the way he used to. I am proud of him, and he has a wonderful wife and children.

Lamina

Lamina is one of my little sisters. When I was with Oliver, we kept in touch with her and supported her. We wanted her to study and leave Gaya for a better future. We even thought we might be able to bring her to Germany. I told her it would be easier if she had the baccalaureate because then she could get a student visa. I had even found a family that was looking for an au pair. All she had to do was go to Bamako to get the documents she needed from the embassy. Oliver and I sent her money, and so did some friends, because I trusted her completely, but as soon as she received the money, she went silent. One day she asked if we could buy her a motorcycle. Oliver and I were very angry because we had opened a door for her. She had a chance to change her life and she did not take it.

Lamina went to Bamako to study and from time to time she called me and told me that she was sick and asked me to send her money to buy medicine. I did, of course. I asked her about the family, because I had no news. I did not know where they were, or anything about them. I wanted her to tell me things about them, and about everyday life in Mali, because I did not know anything. But communications between us gradually petered out. One day, Lisha asked me if I was coming to Lamina's wedding, which was supposed to take place in three days' time. Of course, I couldn't get there that quickly. Sometime later, I saw a picture of her on social media with her baby. She had not told me she had had a child. It was as if I was a stranger. When I asked her why she had not told me, she said, "Because you didn't tell me that you had a baby either." She had seen a picture of me holding someone else's son and had thought it was my child. There could be no reason for me to hide my child if I had one. Lamina ended up breaking off contact with me. I have heard that she is married to the father of her son, who is a wealthy man.

Marlec and Malic

One day when I arrived in Gaya, I saw two little boys who were very cute. I immediately felt a very strong bond between us and said to my sister, "Too bad they are not my little brothers." My sister told me that they were in fact my brothers. That made me very proud. They are non-identical twins and I saw them three or four times during my visits to Gaya. They were born several years after I left for Germany and they too now have a habit of only calling me to ask for money.

Lisha

I have seen Lisha only twice. The first time she was still a baby and the last time she was just a little bit older. She also calls me only to ask for money.

Made in the USA
Middletown, DE
21 April 2023

29271204R00084